Asher

DRAGON'S SAVIOR BOOK 1

KATHI S. BARTON

World Castle Publishing, LLC
Pensacola, Florida
Copyright © Kathi S. Barton 2015
Hardback ISBN: 9781629892856
Print ISBN: 9781629892863
eBook ISBN: 9781629892870
First Edition World Castle Publishing, LLC, June 26, 2015
http://www.worldcastlepublishing.com

Licensing Notes
Cover: Karen Fuller
Cover Model: Alex Stilin
Photographer: Xie4to-graphy
Editor: Eric Johnston
Editor: Maxine Bringenberg

Prologue

Anthony waited in his chambers for the man to be brought to him. He wanted to...well what he wanted to do, very badly, was not going to happen until he was sure that things were taken care of here. And that was what he was waiting on Elbert to help him with. He looked back at the painting on the wall and felt his heart break again. She was gone; his lovely wife was gone from this world, and he'd be joining her very soon if things went the way the course was taking.

"Sire? He's here." Anthony nodded and asked to have him shown to the throne room. "I will, sire. And the young woman is here as well. I have shown her to the sitting room until you are ready for her." Elbert, his ever faithful servant, bowed as he left him there.

Anthony made his way to the young man as soon as he was able to stand on his own two feet. Jacob was his only hope...his last hope that his family line would continue. As he entered the room, he pulled his magic around the two of them tightly, not wanting anyone to hear this conversation. Jacob was kneeling before the chair that Anthony's wife had sat in not hours before when all hell had broken loose. Anthony spoke to the man now kneeling before him.

"I should like to ask you a favor, please. It is more than any man should ask of another, but—"

"Anything, my lord." Anthony actually smiled. He'd expected no less from the man. "You have done more for me and my family than anyone has done for us before. I will be here to serve you for as long as I live."

"You might want to think about this before you say yes, Jacob. What I ask of you is more...it is more than asking you to raise your arms up for me or to put in a bigger crop. This is a matter of life and death for so many people; our linage, mine and yours as well." Anthony asked him to come closer to him so that they may speak.

"Sir?" Jacob looked up, then back at the floor before continuing. "Sir, you wish for me to come to you? Up there? I don't think that is the way things should go, sir. No matter the favor you ask of me."

"I do. I wish for no one to hear what we are speaking about. And should you come closer, I can tighten my magic around us so that no one will." Jacob got up but he moved like a man who was going to the gallows. "I swear to you, Jacob, if you tell me no for the task that I ask of you, I will treat you no differently." There would be no time, he wanted to add, but he didn't. There was no reason to frighten him anymore.

"Perhaps you should tell me then." Anthony smiled again; his face, unused to the movement, ached just a little. His heart was simply too heavy for happiness. "But should you need me to do either of those things, you have but to ask me."

"I know that." Where to begin, he thought. At the beginning. "You know what I am, do you not? I mean, you know that I am not human?"

"I do." Jacob made it sound as if he was silly for asking him. "I believe I have seen you and your wife flying over my crops on more than one occasion. My mother, rest her soul, told us of how you were a fierce person both as a man and beast."

"She would know." Thinking of Jacob's mother, he knew now why the man was as good as he was. "I should like for you to marry."

That got the younger man's attention. "Marry, sir? While I would love to have a wife and children, I have no means to marry. A wife would wish her husband to be able to plant a crop without fear of it being their last, a home that did not leak on her pies, and an oven that did not smoke more than my grandmother did. I have no money, sir, to marry."

"I have such a woman for you. One that will be beside you no matter your house problems. But that will no longer be an issue for you either. I mean to pay you." Jacob said he had no desire to marry for money. "No, I don't mean that. I mean for you to be paid to do a job for me. But you will need a wife to make it...I'm not explaining this very well. Let me being again."

Anthony thought of his own wife, cold below the ground near their children. And the things that she'd done to protect them from the men who had killed her. He needed Jacob and young Sally to help them more than he would ever be able to.

"My wife...my wife has been killed." Jacob looked shocked and told him how sorry he was. "She died keeping our young from harm. From the very men who will come here soon to kill me as well."

"You wish for me to protect you. I shall do my best, sir. I cannot lift a sword like your men, but I can try. I will die trying." Anthony shook his head. "Sir?"

"I need for you and Sally, the woman I have chosen for you, to wed. In doing so, you will sire six sons with her. Each of them will be strong and brave and will help me with my own." Jacob sat down now, his curiosity piqued. "I have six unborn children hidden away. Each son you have, one of my own children will come to. They will be a part of them throughout their lives together. Their lives will be long and great, too."

The door to the chamber was pressed against, and Anthony knew that men were just on the other side. His time was running short. When Jacob stood up and drew his knife, Anthony knew that this man had given him hope where it had not been before.

"I have little time, so listen to me. Sally awaits you in the other room. Elbert will come to stay with you for your life, then remain to care for your sons when they grow. My children will...they will protect your sons as your sons will protect them. Sally has her own magic to give them that will keep them hidden from men like those that are going to kill me. Your job is to raise them up for me. Raise them to be good men and dragons that I would be proud to call my own." Elbert came to him then, the girl he'd chosen for Jacob with him. "Go with her. Elbert will have all you need to be safe and your home cared for."

The door nearly gave way, and he knew it wouldn't hold much longer. Standing up, he nearly shoved the man to his servant and wished them luck. Anthony let his beast take him as soon as his hope for the future was out of sight.

His dragon had been wounded earlier today while he had tried to protect his wife. Now they had come to finish the job, and Anthony was almost ready for them to do so. His children were safe. That was all that mattered for now.

As the men came through the door, their swords raised against him and their fire burning whatever it touched behind them, Anthony sent the last of his magic to his children and told them that he loved them. Then he fought for his own life if only to give their hope, the hope of all their lives, a little more time.

It was over soon, sooner than he'd thought. But he'd lost so much blood, and without his own magic to allow him to fly away, he was hurt over and over until he nearly fell atop those that he'd not managed to kill. And he had killed a great number of them.

The man with the sword came at him, but Anthony had no more strength to move away from the blade as it entered his chest and pierced his heart. As he fell forward, his hot breath killing the last of them, including the man that had taken his life, Anthony knew that all was not lost.

~~~

Jacob held the woman's hand as they ran from the castle. They ran and ran, not even stopping for fallen trees and brambles. He was afraid for them, all of them, having seen the men with the army behind them storming the gate. The king would not be able to keep them at bay for long. He'd known the man was hurt by the blood stain that ran down his chest to his lap.

"I have to rest." He nodded and stopped running to allow Sally to sit on a stump. They'd been running for over an hour, he thought, just running in a direction away from the castle and his home. Jacob looked around and found a few berries to pick and an apple for her. He brought them to the woman. She was holding a tumbler of water when he returned.

"I have magic, did you know that?" Elbert shook his head, then nodded. Her laughter made him think of a spring morning before the dew burned off. "The king wished to ask a favor of me. Did he you as well?"

"He asked me to marry you. Said that we'd have children together. Six sons." She nodded and didn't look the least bit surprised by what he'd said. "I have nothing for us. I told him I barely have a house, but he seemed to think it mattered little."

"It doesn't. Not to me. I can make a fire on the ground if need be. You have shown that you can provide for us today. And you have kept me safe from those men. Men who I'm sure have killed our king." He told her that the queen was dead. "I felt her death as if it were my own. The same men killed her that are now dead in the burning castle."

"He has provided for you both." They looked at the man who had run out with them. Elbert nodded in the direction they were headed. "Ahead, about another day's walk, we will come to a place that is yours. It will provide for you both, and the children you shall have."

"We will live there? For our lives?" Jacob looked at Sally, thinking it was a strange way to word the question. "Or will we sire children only to be put out?"

"Nay, my lady. It will be yours and that of your children when you pass. I will care for them as my own when your time comes. But I assure you, it will be a long while yet. You will not see children of your children born, but you will watch your own grow into men." Elbert took a large satchel from his shirt. "He gave me this to give to you. Should he not have…he knew his time was short, so he had me write what he said. They were coming for him even as he was dying."

"Why?" Jacob sat down, weary himself now. "He was a good king—strong—and kept us safe. He and his wife provided for us and never took more than we could give. Why would they kill them?"

"Because they are human. People…men who have no strength of their own will kill things that they do not understand. The same will be true for your sons someday, I fear." Jacob took the book handed to him and passed it to Sally. He could not read and hoped that she could. "Once you are wed—and I will do the deed for you—things will come to you that you never would have imagined. Beyond the wealth that he has given you, but magic as well. You will need it to protect your children as well as his."

"Why did he choose us?" Jacob nodded. It was a good question from Sally, but Elbert asked if they could walk while he told them. "I would also like to know if we will have daughters too."

"I know not of the other children you will sire. I am sorry. There was no time for much in the way of smaller details." Elbert flushed. "When he gave me this, he lay bleeding, mourning the loss of his wife. But in answer to your question as to why he chose you? It is because you have hearts as pure as the first breath of a child. The wisdom to know right from wrong and stand by it. And he said that he'd never met two people more suited to each other than you. He was quite pleased that you'd remained unmarried until now."

They walked for the rest of the late day. It wasn't until the moon was nearly over their heads that they finally laid down for the night. Jacob laid out his worn jacket for Sally to lie upon, and went to the woods to find things for their fire for the night. He was just coming back when he turned and saw a creature standing on all fours watching over his Sally.

"I am a watcher…what you might call a dog or canine, I suppose." Elbert's voice came from the large Rottweiler sort of creature, and when he turned to look at him, Jacob could see that it was indeed him. "I neither sleep nor eat, young Jacob, but will protect what is in my care. You rest now."

Jacob nodded and moved back to where he'd left Sally. She was lying on the coat, but she was awake. He sat beside her on the cold ground and began stacking the logs for in the morning. She put her hand over his, and he looked at her.

"Are you not happy with our being together, Jacob?" He told her that he had no idea. Her smile made him smile. "You are very honest, aren't you?"

"I see no reason to lie to you. And I won't." She nodded. "Elbert. He's watching us. He's not human, did you know that?"

"Yes." She lay down and patted the place beside her, and he lay with her. "Neither am I; did you know that?"

"He said that you had magic." Jacob put his hand over hers when she put it over his heart. "I will make you happy, I think. I will hope so anyway."

"You have already done so." Jacob looked at her and asked her how. "By not running and screaming into the night when you came upon my father."

It took him several moments to realize she'd meant Elbert. "You are like him? A watcher? I like him, by the way."

"I'm more of my mother. She was magical and my father is as well. We will not live as long as they did, but a long time. Our children will live forever so long as their dragon is safe. Did you read the book that was given to us?" He told her that he couldn't read. "Then I shall teach you. But the book says that our children will be coupled with the dragon on the day that they are born. Once they are together, nothing but death will separate them. And even that bond might be too strong to break then. But they will need each other in ways that we can never understand. It says that their duty is to keep the weak and the overwrought from being killed. That all creatures, human or not, will need them."

She spoke through the night, telling him what she'd read and some of the things that she knew. He listened to her, her voice soothing even when she told him of the trials they'd be put through, raising the children together with dragons. Jacob asked her what he could think of, and when the sun came up over the mountain, he got up from their bed and gathered more wood to start their day. Elbert brought them a skinned rabbit.

After they broke their fast, they started for their new home and new lives. Elbert told them that since they had lain together, he would consider them man and wife. And should anyone ask, they had just married recently.

"Do not tell others where you have been. The castle will be…people will wonder why you have survived when others have not." Jacob agreed, as did Sally. Elbert also told them that should they need anything, anything at all, he would provide it for them. That from now on, they were to try their best to keep to themselves in order to protect the children. All of them.

~~Thirteen months, thirteen days, thirteen hours, and thirteen minutes
after the hour the castle fell~~

The house was filled with the cries of the first born of Jacob and Sally. Asher Anthony Benson came into the world screaming his head off and letting the world know that he had arrived. Elbert took the small bundle from Jacob, who had acted as mid-wife for his own wife, and laid him to rest on Sally's chest.

"He is hungry, I think." Sally pulled him to her breast, and Elbert helped with the clean up as she fed her son. Elbert had never been as proud of anything in his life as to see his first grandchild come into the world.

As Sally lay resting, he picked up young Asher and took him to the porch of the home. Jacob joined him a minute later and the two of them sat on the rockers resting. Sally had had a good labor, short and, with her magic, not too terribly painful. But she needed her rest now and they were glad to give it to her. Elbert looked at Jacob as he handed him his son.

"He will come here soon." Jacob nodded but looked unsure. "The hatchling will not harm Asher, but make him stronger. You know this, correct?"

"I do. But I still worry. The notes that he gave us are very vague as to how they are to be united. It only says they will be as one." Jacob looked at him, then at his child again before continuing. "Will he be a dragon, Elbert?"

"I honestly do not know for sure. What they have done, the king and queen, is something that even I have never heard of. For all we know, he may care for the child himself and never need your assistance again." Jacob looked shocked, and Elbert laughed. He so loved teasing this gentle giant. "Nay, they will both need you. But until he arrives, we will have to wait and see. The next child will be easier, I think. We will know."

Nothing happened the first night, nor the second or third. The baby, young Asher, began to cry more. Nothing would satisfy him. No milk from his mother or a cow would fill his belly. He would kick the blankets off his body no matter how tightly he was bound in them. And he would not allow anyone to hold him for more than a minute or two without screaming again. They all worried for the child.

On the sixth morning, Elbert got up to start his day and knew that something was wrong. There was silence from the babe's room, and the household was warm, too warm for the winter they were coming into. He was just entering the baby's room, shared by his parents, when he heard Sally scream. Elbert knew that the child had died.

He didn't approach the bed that held Asher. Elbert stood back, not wanting to see the vibrant child lying so still in death that he knew had come to him. His heart broke as he heard Sally sobbing and Jacob standing as still as death himself as they stared into the crib. A crib he'd made for the babe himself.

"I shall take him yonder. I am so sorry." Sally turned to him; he could see her tear-streaked face as she put out her hand to him. "Nay. Not yet. My heart...I cannot look upon him just yet."

"He lives." Elbert thought he'd misheard her and asked her to repeat it. "Asher is fine. The dragon has come to him. Come see them."

Elbert walked to the bed slowly, his heart not believing that what his daughter said was true. He was set to bury his first and only grandchild, and she was telling him a falsehood. But when he came to the bed and looked down, he had to blink away the tears several times that clouded what he saw there.

The baby was sleeping soundly, his little arm wrapped around the dragon lying upon his chest. They were of the same size, the two of them, one nearly human child and one fully dragon. Elbert put his hand out to touch them, to assure himself that they were alive, when the dragon lifted his head and hissed at him.

"The book...remember what the book said?" He glanced at Jacob, who had lowered his voice more than likely so as not to wake Asher. "We have to let him have a bit of our blood so that he will know who we are to him."

Sally pulled a small blade from her pocket, the one she used to cut herbs, and sliced it across her finger. Droplets of blood fell from the wound and into the mouth of the tiny dragon. When he nodded at her, she reached in and ran her fingers over the baby and the dragon as well.

"He is warmer than Asher. I wonder that he'd burn him." Jacob cut his finger and let the dragon taste of him as well as Sally continued. "Do you think Asher suffered because his dragon wasn't here?"

Elbert cut his finger then and let the dragon taste of him. But instead of nodding to him, the dragon came up off the baby and landed on his shoulder. He nipped gently at his ear before going back to the bed with Asher.

"What do you suppose he did that for?" Elbert tried not to sound so upset, but the others laughed and he smiled. "He bit me. Do you think because of what I am?"

"No. I think he bit you because you thought him dead." Elbert nodded at Sally at her explanation. "We should leave them now so that they may rest. I think that our lives will be much quieter now that they are together."

Elbert didn't know why, but he thought that this was just the beginning and that their lives would never be quiet again. He hoped he was wrong, but he had a profound feeling that he was right.

Chapter 1

Asher sat behind his desk and tossed the ball he had in his hand to the window again. He was bored, and he needed something to do or he was going to go out and cause some trouble. Asher heard his brother come into his office just as the ball sailed over his head. Smiling, Asher turned to him and leaned back in his chair.

"You do know that the janitor said he would quit if you kept messing with his windows like that." Asher nodded at Jed. "I see. You either don't care if he quits or know that he won't. Which is it?"

"He loves me. So he'll put up with my mess because of that." Jed only snorted as he gave him back the stress ball. "What's going on? Anything I can get into with you?"

"No. I'm going out and I wanted to let you know. The building on Twenty-second is coming down next week and they've run into problems." Asher stood up when he did, and Jed put out his hand. "I'd rather you didn't come with me. You tend to stir the pot when you're on a site."

"I most certainly do stir the pot, and you know how much fun we have when I do that." Jed only shook his head but didn't tell him not to come with him as he made his way to the door. "Who else is going on this adventure with us?"

Asher was the oldest of all the men in his family, with the exception of Elbert, who he was pretty sure was older than dirt. But all kidding aside, when you were as old as they were, all of them, things needed to be stirred up once in a while just so they could get into trouble. And Asher, like his counterpart, loved a bit of trouble once in a while.

His dragon stirred along his skin when they got out into the sunlight. Kiaran was as much a part of him as his skin, and just as important. Asher decided that as soon as he got home tonight, the two of them would play.

The drive over to the building he'd purchased a month ago was made with Jed telling him what the problem was. There were squatters in the building. Not necessarily homeless people—though there were one or two of them in there as well—but people who had not found other homes when they should have.

"How many do we have to displace?" Asher hated to do this, but the building needed to come down now so that they could build the condos that were slated to go in next month. It was not like the building was safe. Most of the plumbing was in bad shape. The wiring was as old as the building, which had been built around the turn of the century, as well as the windows had been broken out on the lower levels long before he'd bought the thing.

"Four, not counting the two homeless people, who are being taken to the housing development on Tenth. They just needed help." Asher nodded. By help, Elam, his brother, meant that they didn't trust that they were being put there free of charge. "I took them there myself and showed them around, and explained that Simeon and Gideon are our brothers and will make sure they're given enough used furniture to start out with, and jobs. The man starts tomorrow at his place, and the woman...well, she's almost too sick to work, but Gideon found her something she can work on at her new home."

"Three of the four are being moved as we speak, but the last one is being difficult." Jed sighed heavily as he continued. "She has a job, means to move herself, but she feels that once she's put in the other house that we'll jack up her rent, double her trash pickup, and she swears that we're going to have all sorts of drug lords move in just to make sure they are never able to sit outside in their yards. She's something else."

Asher had run into this sort of thing before. All of them had, he supposed. Once, about fifty years ago, the six of them had moved into a downtrodden neighborhood to bring it back up to code, and there were several families living in the same house. It had been a chore to make them understand that they really did want to help them, and then more work than any of them imagined just getting them to separate into the homes. There had been nearly twenty-five of them living in a two bedroom flat at that time.

Asher didn't enter the building when they got there. His brother Jed had been working with the families since this began, and it was always best not to introduce a new player when there was trouble brewing. Instead, he leaned back against the limo and let the sun beat down on his face.

I would love to fly. He smiled at Kiaran when he whispered in his mind. *To have the wind blow over my wings, the sun warm my skin. Let the others take care of this and let's go −.*

Asher sat up and looked around when he stopped speaking suddenly. Kiaran was tense, and moved over his body to get a better view. When he pulled from his hand just a little, Asher sat very still while they both scanned the area.

There is a being here that does not belong. Go into the building. Asher stood up and moved toward where his brothers were. But before he was able to take more than a dozen steps, Kiaran lifted from his body and stood in front of him.

Asher didn't move. Not that he'd be able to with the dragon standing in front of him, but Asher knew not to get in his way should there be a fight. He looked around, seeing nothing, but that didn't mean that there wasn't something there. Kiaran rarely showed himself for no reason.

The creature finally appeared, and Asher stared at him. If anyone would have asked him, he would have said that all the trolls were dead. The plague had taken most of them long ago, and the few that had been left had been hunted and murdered. Even some of the very old ones, ones older than Asher himself, had been killed while they slept in their beds. It had been a horrific loss to all beings, but they'd been ill-mannered, bad tempered things from the day they'd been born.

"He wishes a word with you." Asher moved to stand beside his dragon, but didn't take his eyes off the troll. "He claims that there is a prize in the building that he wishes to capture. He thinks that he is deserving of the witch because—and these are his words—he is deserving because he is better looking than you."

The thing in front of him was at least eight feet tall; his face and hands looked like someone had superglued stones and other things that were floating in a creek onto his flesh. His chest, bare of all clothing, was mossy...not the nice, soft green kind, but the moldy type that usually stank as well.

Asher wondered if the man would be able to stand on a scale. He had to weigh at least a ton.

"Ask him if he wants to fight for the witch, or will he simply understand that he's not leaving here with her." Kiaran nodded and repeated what he asked to the troll.

No human could see the troll; or if they did, all they saw was a large man that had on ill-fitting clothing, and they knew that he smelled bad. Asher had the ability to see what his true form was because of his bond with Kiaran. Other supernaturals could see the troll as well, but few of them would mess with him. Asher and Kiaran had fought his kind before.

"He said that he is claiming her." Asher asked him what that meant. "I think he means to use her as his concubine."

Asher didn't want any trouble. Not now. But if need be, he'd kill the troll in order to save the woman. It was their duty to save all mankind, sometimes even from themselves. As he pondered what he should do, the troll took a step toward the building and Asher turned to see what had his attention. Jed and Elam were coming out with four people.

Asher reached into the earth and asked for help. They were more than willing to help him, they told him, and that the troll had trodden on them enough. The ground shifted under the troll's feet, knocking him off balance. Not to the ground, but enough that Kiaran could move toward the troll. Before he was standing upright again, Kiaran had cleared the distance between him and the troll, and was flying just above the ground in front of him. Asher moved toward Jed and the others to keep them out of harm's way when and if anything happened.

Asher, because of his connection to the dragon, knew when he was going to attack. Leaping the last few feet toward the humans, he knocked them to the ground just as heat scorched his back. Jed cried out, but Asher wasn't worried about him as he knew his own dragon would protect him; and if he were to be hurt, he'd heal him as well. Elam helped Asher cover the humans to protect them from harm. It was over in a matter of seconds.

Jed helped him up when the people beneath him began to struggle. His back was on fire, but as soon as Kiaran came to him, he knew that he'd be healed. Keeping his back to the people he had saved, he made sure that Elam was all right too. The spitfire, the one that Asher was sure that they were having the problems with, started poking him in the chest with her finger, yelling at him as soon as she was on her feet.

"You should be whipped for knocking me on my ass. What sort of company do you run that it's okay for men to go around hitting old women to the ground? You're all a bunch of sorry assed morons." Asher looked at Jed and he nodded. "What do you have to say for yourself? Hmm? You like tossing women out on their asses, then knocking them down in the street when they don't want to go? What would your mother think? Or were you born under a rock?"

"My mother would be appalled." Asher tried to dust off the woman's apron, but she smacked him away. "But she'd be more upset with me had I let the building come down around your ears. We told you that the building had to be destroyed, yet you wouldn't leave when you were told to."

"I'm not going to listen to someone that still has a cat lick the fuzz off his face." Asher could have been her great-great-great-grandfather, he thought, but he said nothing as she continued. "In my day we let people die where they wanted. Not tell them they're going in some fancy hotel only to find out that they've been put into one of them assisted living pieces of shit. Have you seen the news about them places? They take your pension, then leave you on the sidewalk to die."

"I doubt very much anyone would take a damned thing from you unless you let them." She stood staring at him, then looked in the direction of where the troll had been. "Did you see him too? Did you know why he was here?"

Asher waited for her to deny it, or at the very least for her to ask him what the hell he was talking about. Instead she looked back at him and nodded. There was a look of fear there, and something more. Asher put his arm around her shoulder and led her to the waiting car.

"He's been stalking me for years. I was...I was able to get away from him for a bit and a day, but he found me a couple of weeks ago. I was afraid to leave the building. He'd get me for sure then. The stupid thing just wouldn't take no for an answer. I'm really glad that you and the others...well, I thank you." Asher helped her into the car and called to Kiaran. As soon as their bodies connected again, Asher felt the burn in his back begin to heal. "You're one of them cops, aren't you? Those kind that come in when you have problems that the humans can't deal with?"

"We help when we can." She nodded and looked up at him from the car seat. "You'll be safe there. I promise you. And there are protections in place that will keep others like him from getting to you."

"I have my own spells to work with, thanks. But I appreciate you helping me out." She looked up at him and smiled. "Just so you know, I have an idea of what you are. But this place you think you're taking me, does it really have two bedrooms in it? I've been wanting to start me a...a craft room. Also...I'm thinking I need a new look. I don't want to attract the wrong kind of element to me. What do you think?"

"Yes. To both your questions. And I've always been a firm believer that you are in charge of your own self. If you want to be different, then by all means, go for it." She nodded and told him she might do just that. "All right. You do that and tomorrow I'll have someone come by and make sure that everything is all right in the apartment. I can't give you any money, but I can give you a fresh start."

"I got me some money." She pulled her skirt up and showed him the money pouches tied to her leg. "You just help with the craft room and stuff and I'll be not bothering you again. Provided that you don't need me some time in the future, which I'm thinking you will."

"Everything I told you is true. And as for needing you, I'm sure you need to keep yourself safe more than you need to help me out. I think I have it under control."

He watched the car move out of the area and turned to his brother. Jed was looking decidedly poleaxed but said very little. The rest of the people were helped into a waiting van and taken to the houses set up for them across town. As soon as everyone was gone, Asher walked over to where the troll had been killed.

"He was going to take the female." Asher nodded at Elam. Casdon and Zak, dragons to Elam and Jed, respectively, were hovering around the scene burning off the residue of the troll. "Do you think she's going to be any trouble? The woman I mean. Do you think she'll be giving us any more trouble at the houses?"

"No. She said she'd been terrified to come out of the building for a few weeks now. She could see that he wanted her. I don't know why she came out with you guys today, unless it was because we were here and there was safety in numbers." Jed shook his head and Asher frowned. "Did she say something to you?"

"Yeah, she said that you were here." Asher asked Jed what the hell that meant. "Don't know, but when we were telling her that she needed to leave, she was standing at the window. Then she asked who you were. I told her my brother and she asked me if you were the oldest. As soon as I told her you were, she was ready to go right away."

Elam didn't know either but confirmed that she was ready and willing after that. "Jabbered on and on about the second bedroom at the new house, but nothing more about you. And she never mentioned the troll. When we came out of the building, I couldn't believe what I was seeing."

Asher couldn't either but didn't say anything more. There were workmen coming on site now that the building was empty. As soon as the movers came out with the last of the things that the few tenants had left, big engines were started up and they roared to life tearing down the building.

Asher made his way home shortly after the workers had most of the building down and were quitting for the day. Usually he would walk home, enjoying the day, but he got into the limo and sat in the back with his eyes closed. If he was honest with himself, and he rarely was, he wasn't bored. Asher was exhausted.

He had been born over three thousand years ago. Jedidiah, or Jed as he liked to be called, was born exactly thirteen months, thirteen days, and thirteen minutes later. Each of them had been born in the same time; their births the same as the dragons that they each held. After Jed had been born, Elam...then Shane, Gideon, and Simeon. Their dragons, in order of their births, were Kiaran, his own dragon; Zak belonged to Jed; and Casdon, Keion, Onimia, and Akassa to the others. Their names, each of them knowing them before they were born, meant a special power that was given to them while their parents were alive.

As soon as he got to his home, he told Elbert that he was going to bed. Before going up to his room on the top floor, he let Kiaran go and then left the door open from the balcony to allow him to come in when he was finished flying. Asher stripped down to his bare skin and crawled into the big bed.

~~~

Elbert was worried for the young man. Asher had been restless of late, and when he got that way, usually he could go away for a few years and come back rejuvenated. Elbert didn't think that would work this time. The man didn't need to get away, but to become involved.

"He needs a good woman." Elbert didn't turn to look at the man standing behind him. Jacob visited him still after all these years, even though he should have gone on to be with his lovely wife in the afterlife.

"She would murder him the first time she saw the way he keeps his office. I've never known a man that took after his father so much as he has." Jacob laughed, and Elbert turned to look at his old friend. "You have been away for a long time this time. Where did you go?"

"Looking." They both sat at the table. Jacob could no longer touch or taste things, but he loved to smell them, and Elbert loved to find things, small items that had a wonderful odor to them, for Jacob. He pulled his little treasure box down from the top of the refrigerator now.

Elbert was holding out the bar of soap he'd found in a market place a few weeks ago when he decided to tell him what he knew about young Asher. The man was his father, but had been gone longer than he'd been in his life. Elbert had hated to see them both go, Sally and Jacob, but loved the fact that they had died together one night; simply fell asleep, never to wake.

"Asher is looking for trouble, I think. Danger that has gotten him injured badly a few times." Jacob asked to smell the tea bag that Elbert had found at the corner café, but said nothing else. "Even Kiaran is worried for him. Last week they were both laid up for nearly a day, just resting from a fight they'd been in."

"He fought a troll today. Kiaran killed him, but I think that Asher would have gone ahead of him had the dragon not stepped in." Elbert nodded. He knew that Jacob sometimes walked with his sons, but he never spoke to them. Elbert wasn't even sure that he could. "I, too, fear for him. And Kiaran. They are both much alike."

When the things were looked over, Elbert put the empty box back and tossed out the things that had been in it. He would not use the things he'd found. They were only for the dead man that spoke to him now. Elbert neither ate nor slept, so had no use for a chocolate chip cookie or a bag of tea. When he sat back down, he looked at Jacob.

"I have found him a mate." Elbert didn't say anything. He knew that Jacob and Sally had had great powers, but had never figured them all out. If Jacob said he found a mate for his eldest son, then he more than likely had. "She is sort of human, as I was, but she is…I think her suited for my son. Her temper is high and she has a mouth on her that might get her into trouble a little, but she will be a match to Asher's temper."

"Asher has no temper that I know of." Jacob smiled and Elbert got it. "You mean her temper will give him one. And you think this is a good thing? That our mild Asher have a woman that will test him?"

"I do. He is much too sedate, I think you call it. Bored, he has told his dragon. I've never been bored a day in my life or death. There are many things that...did you know that there is a train that will go faster than anything on earth? Well, perhaps not that fast, but it was so much fun to watch it zoom by me." Jacob laughed. "And the smells from some of the vendor stalls in New York. Had we had such a place when I was alive, I would have tried a new dish each night. All this is out there, and all Asher and the others do is work and make more money. Do they not have enough yet?"

Elbert had often thought the same thing, but it was not his place to say so. Instead he asked Jacob about the troll. This took an hour of his time and gave Elbert time to think as well. He was worried about all his grandsons, but Asher the most.

"He does not see anyone—not after that woman—does he?" Elbert told him no. "I wanted to warn him what she was about, but I'm not sure he would have listened. She was a viper, that woman. Not suited to him at all."

"She has been gone a long time. How long do you think him to mourn her?" Jacob told him he wasn't mourning her, but he'd had his heart broken and was not going to let anyone close again. "Then how will you get him with his mate? You said that she has a temper. But we both know that Asher is the most stubborn of them all. When he has his mind set, whether it be good or bad for him, he will not stop until he has lost or won."

"I have a plan." Elbert wanted to roll his eyes. Jacob with a plan was a disaster. It always had been. He nearly pointed out the last plan he'd had but didn't. The kite that he'd tried to use to bring electricity into the house was still a charred mess in the tree by their ancestral home. He was sure that he could do it. And the children, all six of them, had cheered him on. Right up until the barn had caught fire.

"I think you need a vacation." Elbert raised a brow at Jacob. "Take Asher home with you. Go on out and see mine and Sally's graves. Lay us a few flowers on them. Sally would love that from her boy. Then we'll see how my plan works out."

"She's at the house now?" Jacob said nothing but only smiled. "Why do I have the feeling that you're going to upset him more than he is now? He's on the edge, Jacob. What if something happens to her and he never finds her again?"

"Then you should hurry." Jacob started to fade out, and Elbert nearly called him back when he came back on his own. "Oh. I forgot to mention to you, she's a mite on the stubborn side herself, and a tad mad at me."

Elbert sat there for a long time after Jacob left. When he saw him next time, Elbert decided, he was going to not give him the box of treats. And he'd be on the lookout for something grand too. Just to tease him with.

Chapter 2

"I appreciate you coming out here with me. I have not been back in a while." Asher nodded but said nothing. It was just as well he'd left home. It was that or he'd have to murder one of his brothers for not letting him be himself…which to say was his stubborn self. "The house should be completed by now."

"I should hope so." They'd hired a crew to come to the house nearly a year ago to upgrade the entire thing. Electric and plumbing had been put in years ago, but it needed to be made safe. Plus it needed to be painted and new carpets put in. They had even decided to have new windows put in just as an extra measure, with a new furnace and air conditioner as well. "Do you think that the mess is cleared away by now? Elam said the last time he was here, which was a couple of months ago, that the big dumpsters were full and they'd been putting the trash near it until one could be replaced. They said that would be another month."

"The weather." Asher nodded. The weather was always a factor in getting to the house. There were no real roads to get in and out of the place. And when it was nice to get in and out, a freak storm could keep them there for a week if the creek overflowed. "When you were just a wee one, your mother took a walk to the mushroom patch she'd been watching. While she was there, a storm came in and flooded everything, including her path to come home."

"Kiaran brought her home. I had forgotten about that." There were a great many things he'd forgotten, and the ride to their home was bringing a lot of them back. "Mom loved it out there. I'm really glad that she and Dad are buried there. I miss them."

"As do I."

Asher knew that his father came to see Elbert. He'd never seen him but knew he was there, and Asher had always thought it was because of the magic that they had shared. He missed his dad—his wit and his common sense—and wondered what he'd think about his behavior lately. His mom would have whipped the tar out of him, and Kiaran too for letting him get into so much trouble.

As soon as the house came into view, Asher felt the last several months of stress fall off his shoulders. Even Kiaran stretched out, and he put his hand out the window to allow the dragon his freedom. As he soared to the skies, his wings spreading out over the bright blue sky, Asher looked at the house.

From the outside it looked no different than it had when he was a boy. The weathered boards were dark with age, the windows were new, of course, but the shutters, the kind that actually fit over the windows, were there to use in the stormy months. The second and third stories had wraparound porches on them, like the lower level, and each of the rooms spilled out onto their own section of it for a bit of privacy. He nearly leapt from the car when it came to a stop.

Going in the house was both painful and wonderful for him. Memories, all of them good, seemed to cascade around him like a well-worn blanket. He could snuggle into them as if he could wear them and never leave again. He looked at Elbert when he came in burdened with their luggage. Taking his own and the other man's, he took them up the stairs and put them in the rooms that had always been theirs. He stopped by his parents room to look in, and felt the weight of their death like it had only just happened.

Bags of food were sitting on the counter when he came back down. Putting away some of the foodstuff, he realized how much Elbert had brought with them.

"How long are we staying?" Elbert didn't answer him, and Asher felt that he'd been tricked. "Elbert?"

"I thought you could use a vacation. I know that I could." Asher only waited. He knew this man as well as he did himself and something was up. "I want to clear away some of the weeds in the garden while I'm here, and take a few herbs back with me. Then there are the graves. No one has cleaned them off in a good long time, and what would your mother say?"

"And?"

Elbert only shrugged and Asher wanted to ask again. But he turned to him then and Asher could see the sadness there.

"I should like to go to the castle ruins as well." Asher nodded. He'd never been there himself—none of them had been allowed when they were younger, and as they grew older...well, no one had ever suggested it again. They had always feared that someone would know what they were and who they held to them. But he knew that Elbert had gone several times, as well as their father before his death.

35

As soon as he finished putting away the groceries with Elbert, Asher went out onto the porch. As soon as he sat down, Kiaran landed with a soft thud in the yard. Asher was still amazed every time he saw him, and how handsome he was as a man. Seldom was he able to be whichever he wanted, unless they were on this magical ground.

Kiaran, like his brothers, was not the largest of dragons ever born. In fact, they were only a little bigger than Asher was. Elam's was a little taller, but the rest of them were about seven feet tall.

They were all a beautiful mixture of greens and brown. Kiaran told him once that it was so that he could blend in should he not have a chance to make himself invisible. Asher didn't know if that was true or not since the dragon could pull shadows around himself faster than he could blink.

The wings on each of them were a little different. Kiaran's were a dark green, almost the color of moss that had seen very little sun. They were wider than they were long but still touched the earth when they were curled behind him as they were now. But it was his face that made Asher think of beauty, if a male dragon could be called beautiful.

His face was long, as one would expect on a dragon. His teeth on his upper jaw hung long over his lower lip and were sharp as razors. He had several horns on his head; mostly they were for fighting, except for the one that was in the center of his head. That one was to kill.

It could stretch from his head to be two feet long when needed. He'd never seen him use it on anyone, but Asher had seen him show it off to something they'd be fighting. And over the years, all the centuries they'd been together, he thought he and Kiaran had killed more beings than all of the rest.

It was their job, he supposed, killing off the rogues or bad things that haunted those that could not fend for themselves. It was a job they all took very seriously…that and making the family wealthy. Actually, they'd been very well to do long before they'd been born to his parents. The king had indeed provided for them very well. But they'd added to their fortune over the years, and now they would never have to work again, should they not want to.

"You look several hundred years younger." Asher nodded, not moving his feet when the dragon came up on the porch with him and shifted from beast to man. It still, to this day, startled him to think that not every being in the world had a dragon with them at all times. "Shall I tell you what I have found? Or do you wish to go exploring on your own?"

"I want to relax for a little while first. If it's nothing dangerous, then I could care less at the moment." Kiaran told him all was safe. "Then no, I'll rest for a little while. I guess we're going to be here for more than a few days. Elbert wants to see the castle ruins and see to Mom and Dad's graves."

"I should as well. Will you go with us?" Asher said he didn't know just yet. "You should go. It's nearly all grown over now. Not much there but a wall and a lot of stones. I have often thought of going there to find something of my fathers. Do you suppose that would be possible? I mean we'd have to move a few of the larger pieces, but I would like to try."

"I don't know why not. The castle burned to the ground the night that he was killed, right?" Kiaran nodded. "The stone would have fallen in on it at some point, but with your strength you could lift a few out of the way to have a better look, as you said."

"I think I may go to see where she hid us away as well." Another place that Asher had never been allowed to go. He told him he would go with him there. "My mother would have protected us with her body. I don't remember much about the place from when I left it to come to you that day, but I should like to go back there now."

As the two of them started walking toward the mountain, Asher thought of his childhood here. There had never been a time when he'd had friends over. There simply weren't any to be had. But he'd had his brothers and their dragons to play with, and it had been more than enough. His dad had made learning an adventure for them as well. Mom had taught their dad to read, as well as them, and Dad in turn had shown them how to survive in the world. Over the centuries it had served them well, and he made sure that he said as much to Elbert so that he could pass it on to their father.

"Did you know that Dad speaks to Elbert?" Kiaran said that he did. "I thought you might. Do you think the others know?"

"My brothers know, but yours do not." They were almost to the mountain when Kiaran stopped him. "I should tell you that one of the things I have found out here is in there. The second opening to the left. I think she lives there when there are people in the area."

"She?" Kiaran nodded. "You mean a person lives in the mountain? Why on earth would she do that? Doesn't she know that this is private property?"

"I believe your dad told her she could stay here." He asked him how he knew that. "She has seen him recently. His scent is near the cave but not on her. She is well, but not healthy. I do believe that she will die this year should the weather turn bad enough. The food that she eats is plentiful, of course, but she's not good at picking things to keep her well."

Asher wondered how old the woman was and whether or not she was human. There had been others around, humans that had come here thinking to find something. Something to make a quick buck off of. The legend of the dragon tears had been around as long as he had. Probably longer.

It was true to an extent. Dragon tears did turn to diamonds. Some of them did anyway. But that wasn't all they turned to. Sometimes there were rubies and opals, even a few times he'd seen emeralds as well. Kiaran could also produce gold when he wanted, just by simply running his clawed hand over a riverbed or creek. The tears and the gold were what had kept them in pocket money their entire life.

"We'll have to see that she gets medical help then. Maybe we can get her into a nursing home nearby. They're better at keeping someone like her healthy than living in a cave could." Kiaran said nothing as they started up the hill. "When we get back to the house, I'll tell Elbert to have her removed. I don't want her dying in there. Something might get at her."

"If you wish." It was a strange thing to say, even for a dragon. Before he could ask him what he meant, something was shoved in the back of his head. "I do believe that your elderly woman got the drop on you."

"Who the fuck are you and what the fuck are you doing on my mountain?" Her voice was full of hatred, and Asher started to turn to talk to her. "Move and I'll blow your head off."

"Well?" He had hoped that Kiaran would help him, but he only smiled and shrugged. "I thought you were supposed to protect me."

"If you think you need it from her, then I will. But I do believe that you can take her." Asher started to turn again, but she hit him with whatever it was she had at his head. "She isn't going to be reasonable, I think."

"I'm not going to be the one with a bullet in my head if you don't get the hell out of here." Asher closed his eyes and tried to think what to do as the woman hit him again. Enough was enough and he turned and ducked at the same time. The gun went off very close to his ear, and he saw Kiaran shift and take off for the skies. It was the perfect distraction he needed to take care of the woman.

But the moment he saw her, he froze in place. And since he was the one that was now off balance, she hit him again and he went tumbling back. Grabbing out for something, he touched the girl's arm and pulled her with him. Her cry of pain echoed his as he hit his head on a stone when he hit the earth. Then nothing.

~~~

Elbert stood over the two of them and watched them carefully. Had Kiaran not helped him bring them to the house, he wasn't sure what he might have done to get them here. Neither of them had moved in the hour they'd been there, and he was beginning to worry.

"You worry overly much." Elbert glared at Jacob. "But you just look at them together and tell me that they're not matched perfectly."

"They are unconscious, sir. I don't think that this is the time to play matchmaker with them. Besides, the woman is very hostile if you ask me." Elbert did think she was quite pretty. "What was she doing in the cave anyway? You said she was living here."

"I was living here but heard you guys coming up the road." The woman sat up and glared at the two of them. Then she looked at Asher. "What the hell was he doing trying to attack me? And that guy with him? Did I really see him fly off?"

"Yes you did." Elbert handed her an ice pack that had fallen to the floor when she sat up. "I have made sure that you are all right, but I think you need to rest for a bit longer."

"So? We're just going to skip over the part where that guy was flying around?" Neither he nor Jacob answered her, and she stood up. "I'm going to go back to where I was staying, if you don't mind. I have —"

"You're not going anywhere." Elbert knew that Jacob was gone the moment that Asher spoke. "What the hell were you thinking when you tried to shoot me?"

Asher held onto her arm when she started to get up, and Elbert backed up. He was an immortal, yes, but the young woman looked like she'd make him wish for a quick death. Asher stood up and pulled her with him. The two of them did seem to sort of fit. Like they were a matched pair of tempers too.

"You attacked me, you overgrown asshole. And what were you doing with the flying guy? Don't think I didn't notice that shit either. People popping in and out all the time." She turned to him, and Elbert backed up again. "What are you running here? A circus?"

"I don't think so." He was confused. Not that it wasn't unusual for him to be in that state, but he was also nervous and he was having a hard time holding his shape. "Perhaps this would be better if we had cooler heads."

Kiaran chose that moment to come into the room. While the dragon wasn't large, he was a little intimidating when there were already high tempers. As soon as he moved to Asher, to no doubt blend with the man, the woman attacked. And Kiaran, being a protector, retaliated. Elbert let his human shape go then, and dropped to all fours to get ready for whatever he needed to do.

No one moved. Elbert wasn't sure right then if that was a good thing or not, but the woman came toward him with her hand out. She was trembling, and as much as he hated to admit it, he felt like it was his fault.

"He won't bite." Going to his belly, Elbert looked at Asher, hoping he'd explain something to the woman before she came any closer. "Just don't try to shoot him. He's an immortal like me, and he might just tear your arm off."

"Fuck you," the woman said, then went to her knees in front of Elbert and smiled. Elbert sat up, his ass still sitting on the floor, and cocked his head at her. "You're a pretty boy, aren't you? What are you?"

"Elbert is a shifter, but he prefers to be this guy. He's a Rottweiler. The first of his kind." The hand at his head had him turning to her again. Asher continued to speak but Elbert didn't care anymore. She was petting him and scratching him behind the ear as the children had when they were smaller. "We're not humans, so I'd not screw around with us and get the hell off our property."

"Is he always so friendly?" Elbert shook his head and she laughed. He could see right then what had attracted Jacob to her. "Well, Mr. Elbert, if he gives you any shit, you can come and stay with me. I love dogs of any kind. It's assholes that I don't like."

When she stood up and looked at Asher, Elbert could see that he was pissed. It wasn't a mood he'd seen on the younger man in a very long time. When she made her way to the door he followed, just wanting to make sure that she was going to be all right. But Asher got to her first.

"Where the hell do you think you're going?" She tried to dodge him again, and he put his hands on her arms. When she cried out in obvious pain, he pushed her to the bed and ripped her shirt sleeve up. "Who did this?"

Elbert was able to shift back then, and he left the room to get the first aid kit. It had come in handy over the centuries, and had been updated just recently when he'd brought it with him the last time he'd been here checking on things. When he returned, the young woman was arguing with Asher, and Elbert was beginning to think this was going to be an ongoing thing with these two.

"I said it's just fine. Will you...what the hell are you doing now?" Kiaran was standing next to the table now, but he was a man, not a dragon. He looked concerned, and Elbert knew that it was more than just a bad cut. He asked him what it was.

"It's from a witch. She's been cut by her fingernail or a dirty blade." Asher leaned in and sniffed the wound, much to the dismay of the woman. Kiaran continued talking, but Elbert had a feeling it was more to the woman than them now. "Did you meet someone here? Maybe someone that might have asked you a few questions? Like about the people who live here?"

"Yes. But I didn't know anything other than the old man that said I could stay here. But I didn't tell her that." The woman started shaking then, and he could tell it was taking a great deal out of her. "I don't think I feel so well."

"You don't." Asher picked her up and sat her on the counter in his bathroom. "I need to cool you down before I can seal this wound."

He was pulling at her clothing when she smacked his hands away. "What the hell is wrong with you now? Damn it all to hell and back. I don't even know you, and if you think I'm going to hop in the shower with you, naked, you're nuttier than that old woman was. I'm out of here."

"You leave here and by nightfall you're going to be dead." It wasn't said as a threat, but calmly and with a great deal of conviction. The woman turned to Asher as he continued. "She's poisoned you. I don't know if it was on purpose or not, but knowing you, it was more than likely the latter. The way that you're feeling right now, it's shaky, right? And you feel like you're going to throw up. And your toes burn, as do your fingers."

"Yes." Asher put her back on the counter, but she didn't fight him. "How do you know that? Are you a doctor?"

"No. I've been around for a long time." He pulled her shirt off and tossed it on the floor. "My dragon's name is Kiaran. My name is Asher, Asher Benson. And you know Elbert."

"I'm Essie Hahn. Esmeralda really, but no one calls me that." She leaned her head on Asher's chest and Elbert looked at him. There was worry there, more than he'd thought with such a small wound. "I'd like to go to sleep now. If you don't mind taking me back to the cave, I'll rest."

"Maybe later, Essie." He closed his eyes before he spoke again. "We're going to have to burn this, honey. It's bad and the poison is going to kill you."

"Okay." When Asher lifted her head, Elbert got a look at her eyes. They were fevered and she was not focusing on him. "You're very handsome, did you know that? And your mouth looks so kissable. Do you think you could kiss me? Just once."

"I'd rather heal you first." Her lower lip came out and Asher laughed. "You should do that when you're healthy. I'll give you whatever you want then."

Kiaran went into the bathroom with them. Essie had on her bra and her pants but nothing else. Asher was speaking to Kiaran in low tones, but Elbert had no trouble hearing him. They were going to have to hurt the girl before she was going to be able to get better.

When the dragon was standing beside them, Elbert went to get towels and blankets. He heard her scream even from the lower levels of the house, and then he heard Asher cursing. When he got back to the bedroom, Asher was in the shower with the woman and Kiaran was gone.

As soon as Asher and Essie got out of the stall, he met him there with the towels. She was shaking hard enough that Elbert was afraid Asher was going to drop her. Stripping her down to her bare skin, Asher then dried her and wrapped her in a sheet. Then he put her in the bed and took off his own clothing.

"She's been marked. Kiaran thinks he's gotten all the poison out, but he went to get some herbs that grow on the mountain to make a poultice for her." When he was naked, he crawled into bed with her. "My body heat will keep her from getting sick. And when Kiaran returns, he'll join my body and heat us both up for her."

"I'll put some broth on. When she wakes, she'll need it." Asher nodded and pulled Essie into his arms. His hiss made him think she was cold and he asked him.

"No. She's burning up. I'm worried. All that fighting with us, it made the poison run through her system quicker. I don't...for some stupid reason I like this woman." Elbert told him he did as well. As he was leaving the room so that she could rest, Asher called him back. "She saw Dad, didn't she? I mean, that's the old man that let her stay here."

"He told me that he'd met her here. It's why I came up here." Asher nodded but said nothing more. Elbert left the room, leaving the window open for Kiaran to return by.

Chapter 3

Asher pulled the softness to him tightly. He'd never had a pillow that was so lumpy before, and decided that the next time he was in town, he'd look into getting a new one. But when something hit him in the face, he opened one eye and looked at the furious woman in the bed with him. And just like that, the entire ordeal with her came back to him.

"If you pout for me now, I'd be willing to give you that kiss you wanted." Essie huffed at him and struggled to get out from under him. "You have on nothing but a sheet and I have on less than that. If you get up, one of us is going to get a very nice view of the other."

"Where are my clothes?" He pointed to the dresser across the room. There were no clothes in it that were hers, but she didn't have to know that. "And you're naked in bed with me why?"

Asher felt his cock stretch and ache to show her just why they needed to be naked. Instead of telling her, he rolled her to her back and settled between her legs. The blanket he was under had long since been tossed to the floor, and he was hoping that she'd not notice, not yet at any rate. She stared up at him while he pulled her arms above her head. Her legs moved over his, and he nearly missed her intent to unman him.

"You are the most violent woman I know." She tried again, and he put both her hands into his one and then cupped her ass hard to him with the other. Essie stilled, and he watched her mouth when she licked her lips. "You're very beautiful when you're all tossed like you are."

"You're not going to have sex with me." He grinned at her, and she cursed. "Is everything a joke with you? I want you to let me up right—"

Him rocking into her softness had them both moaning. Asher wanted her, wanted to be buried deep within her right now. Holding her to him, he let go of her hands and ran his fingers down her right arm to her chest. Her breast was covered, but the sheet was slipping away. He slipped his fingers under the hem of it and brushed them over her tight nipple.

"Can I taste you? I'd like to just kiss you, but the thought of suckling at your breast makes my cock hurt to be inside of you." Her tongue ran along her lips again, and he leaned in to chase it. She tasted of sweet honey, and he wanted more. Kissing her, deepening the kiss, gave him the opportunity to pull the sheet down and bare her lovely breast for him. Cupping it in his hand, he toyed with her nipple as he explored her mouth.

"Please?" She begged him when he lifted his head to take her breast into his mouth. "Please don't...don't...stop."

He knew that wasn't what she meant, for him not to stop, but he wanted her. Leaning his head down to her breast, he licked her tip while he watched her face. When her body rocked up to his, her breast filling his mouth, Asher pulled the sheet the rest of the way off her body.

Looking down the length of her, what he could see with his body over hers, he felt his mouth water to not just taste her but to nibble on her everywhere. When he suckled at her breast again, she wrapped her ankles over his thighs, and Asher knew that all he'd have to do was push forward just a little and he'd be inside of her. But he didn't want their first time to be over so quickly.

Rolling to his back, he took her with him. She straddled his hips and his cock was stiff in front of her. When she wrapped her fingers around him, bringing her pussy flush with his cock, Asher held onto her hips while she rode him.

"Come for me." She moaned and rode him harder. Sitting up, he pulled her ass to him, lifting her up enough that the next time she came down, he was going to take her. But she wrapped her fingers over him again and lifted her body from his and held him to her pussy. "If you take me inside of you, I'm going to come. I want you to come first."

"I'm coming apart the moment you're inside of me. And I'm going to scream." He held her, trying to catch his breath at the thought of her coming around him. "Asher, please don't tease me. Fuck me."

He pulled her down hard, impaling her on his cock. She was right, as soon as he entered her, he felt her tighten around him and she screamed out her release. Asher let her ride him, giving herself as much pleasure as she wanted, his body hard for his own release. As soon as she started her ride a second time, he rolled her to her back and fucked her as hard as he could, knowing it was going to be the most powerful climax he'd ever had.

She was rolling her hips up to meet his every stroke. Christ, he wanted to come inside of her, release his cum deep within her, but he didn't want it to end. He wanted to be with her, fucking her like this for hours and hours. But she grabbed his ass as she lifted her hips up higher, and he felt his cock being milked by her pussy when she came again. Asher pounded her harder, his cock filling even as his balls emptied deep inside of her. Throwing back his head, Asher cried out his climax, rolling over his entire body with hers.

Her arms dropped from his shoulders, and he felt her hot breath on his neck when he lowered his head to her breast again. Christ, he'd only meant to have some fun with her, but this was more than he'd bargained for. Lifting his head when she said his name, he wanted to take her again. She was simply too beautiful to resist.

"You're heavy." He rolled over again, taking her with him. But she laid over him this time. Asher felt his cock stretch again, and she glared at him. "Men don't come twice."

"I will with you." He fucked her gently, taking his time, bringing her back up again. "You have the most beautiful body. Hard in all the right places, soft in others. I love the way your breasts feel against me. And your nipples are beautiful, all red from my mouth. Let me taste them again. I want to nibble on them until you come." She lifted her breast to his mouth, and he did just what he wanted. Her moaning had him fucking her harder until she was panting with him.

"You're a very smooth talker, and you keep that up, and I'm going to come again." He told her he hoped they both would. "I want to ride you again. I love watching your face when you fuck me like that."

He helped her to sit up, and she swung her leg over him and stood next to the bed. He had no idea what she'd been planning to do, but she stood staring at him. Asher didn't move. Few people had ever seen him like this. He didn't hide his dragon from her so he knew just what she was seeing. Even those that did see him ran from him when they did.

"Does it hurt?" Kiaran moved but didn't leave him. Essie put her hand over where his head was and then the dragon lifted up. Not from his body but enough that she could feel him. "He's really a part of you."

"Yes." She moved closer to the bed, and he put his hand on her ass and pulled her even closer. "When you touch him, I feel it too. Rub his head and watch my hair."

As she did as he'd asked, he felt her fingers run over his hair and knew that his hair ruffled with her movements. Asher had never had anyone study him so intently before, and wasn't sure what to do when she sat on his lap again.

"Does he have sex with me when you do?" He told her no. Kiaran was a dragon that could only have sex with his mate. "But he's here. With us."

"He can feel you when you think of him. If you...say his name and he will part from my body to come to your call." Asher waited for her to do that, but she only stared at him. When her fingers touched his chest, running along his body, he felt the dragon purr, something he'd never done before. "He likes what you're doing. Can you hear him?"

He didn't think she could. In fact he was sure of it. But when she said that she could hear him purring too, Asher sat up. He put his hands under her breasts and held them to his mouth. Suckling one, then the other, he tried to tell himself that it didn't mean anything that she could hear his dragon.

"I want to come with you again." He pulled her closer to him, her pussy hard against his abdomen as he helped her ride him. "I'm so close. I never...sex usually doesn't mean anything for me."

"I want to drink from you." She moaned, and he turned her onto the bed. Standing next to it, he moved her legs off the edge and sat on the floor between her thighs. "Christ, do you have any idea how much I'd like to fuck you again?"

"Yes." Asher lifted her legs and put them up on his shoulders. He didn't want anything in his way when he started eating her, and he wanted to do it right now. Leaning into her, he didn't know that once he did start that he'd ever want to quit. Licking her from gate to clit, then sucking the hard nubbin into his mouth, he felt her legs tighten around him as she screamed out her release again.

Asher brought her three more times before she pulled his head up by yanking his hair. He crawled up her then, tasting her flesh as he went, biting her gently where he could. Holding his cock in his hand, he rubbed it over her swollen clit and watched her face as he did it. She was close again, and he wanted to fill her when she came.

Sliding into her, he moved slowly. But she wasn't having that and wrapped her legs around his hips and rose up to meet his downward strokes with a hard thrust of her on. When her fingers cupped his ass, pulling him into her deeper, Asher moved deeper and then deeper still, watching her face as she came again. She begged him to join her, crying out that she wanted to feel him come inside of her, and Asher came hard, pounding her through two more climaxes as he emptied into her.

Dropping on top of her, he rolled to his back, taking her with him once again. Sleep was hard coming on him, and he wrapped his body around hers as she slept. He had a feeling that she was going to leave him as soon as she woke, and he really didn't want that to happen. Asher had no idea why, but the thought of her leaving him, and not just his bed, made him think that harm would come to her. Maybe to them both.

~~~

Essie sat on the floor after trying and finally succeeding to get out from under Asher for ten minutes. It was exhausting trying to move a big body off you, she thought, when all you wanted to do was have him wake up and take you again. Christ, the man had made her feel like she'd never felt before, during or even after sex. She looked up when she heard a noise.

The big dragon only stared at her. She was actually a little afraid of him, but he moved a little and was suddenly a man. He sat in the chair near the window and leaned back as if he had not a care in the world.

"I helped you." She looked at Asher, then back at him. "He would have awakened the first time you moved if I hadn't made him sleep harder. I wanted to talk to you."

"About what?" She started to stand but realized that she only had the sheet she'd managed to snag and nothing else. "He said my clothes were over there. Can you hand them to me?"

"The clothing you had on has been burned. I thought it better to have all traces of the witch out of this house. It turns out I was correct, as there was enough of her power on them to have let her past the protection. But I want to talk to you about Asher." She nodded, guessing that since he held all the cards for now, she'd listen. "You and he, did you know that it was planned that you come together?"

She stared at him, wondering what he was talking about, and said nothing. But her mind was trying to wrap around trying to come up with why the hell anyone would want her. When she thought of something, Essie realized that he hadn't said anything either.

"If you're warning me off him, I can tell you now that it was just sex. I don't know where you got your information, but I assure you, I don't need nor want a man in my life. Especially one that has dragons as part of his body and a man who shifts into a dog." She started to stand, hurt more than she could say that this guy was turning her away. "I'm not sure where...you know what, I don't really care if you like me or not. I was doing just fine before you two came to the cave."

"You weren't surprised about him having a dragon. Nor that Elbert was a shifter. Why not?" She stood up then, not really caring if she was naked or not, and dragged the sheet from under Asher to wrap around her. "You were sent here to spy on him, on all of them, weren't you?"

Essie could have told him that the man Jacob told her. She'd actually thought him off his rocker a little, but he'd been kind enough to offer her the barn to sleep in, and she thought she could put up with a lot for a dry place to sleep for a change. Walking to the big dresser that was near the bathroom, she opened the top drawer to find the neatest stacks of underthings she'd ever seen. Taking out a pair of the silk boxers, she went to the next one to find herself a shirt. There was no way she'd be able to wear any pants of the person this room belonged to, so she didn't bother. Dropping the sheet to dress, she let the tears fall as she spoke to Kiaran, beyond caring if he was embarrassed or not.

"The man, Jacob, told me about him. All of you actually. Not that it matters, but he let me sleep here until spring. I'm not going to now. As for you warning me off your friend, fuck you." She jerked the shirt over her head after pulling on the too large boxer shorts. "As for you warning me away, well, thanks. I'm so glad that he has someone looking out for him that is just as much an asshole as he is."

Essie started to the door and thought for sure he was going to stop her. When she opened it and stepped into the hall, she nearly ran but didn't want to give him the pleasure of seeing how badly he'd hurt her. And for the life of her, Essie had no idea why his rejection of her hurt so badly. It's not like she'd not been rejected before.

Elbert was standing in the kitchen when she entered. Jacob was there as well, and he stood up when she started for the door. He stepped in front of her before she could leave.

"What's happened?" Before she could answer, Kiaran spoke behind her, telling Jacob to let her go. "I will not. She's been crying. What did you say to her? Where is my son?"

"That fucking prick put him in a deeper sleep so I could be tossed out." The words hurt even herself, but she didn't care. "I'd very much like it if you moved the hell out of the way, Mr. Jacob. I've got somewhere else to be."

She got the door opened and was tossed back so hard that she hit her body against the wall across the room. The heat, blistering and consuming, touched every part of her, and she knew that she was dead. Hands pulled at her. Essie tried to get away but the pain was too much. Suddenly she was wrapped up and the pain was gone.

"Breathe." She nodded, not sure what was going on, but she was told to breathe again and again. "You're burned badly, but if you'll just give me a few more minutes, I'll have you healed."

When he released her, she realized who'd held her. Backing away from Kiaran, she bumped into a large body behind her. When he touched her arms, there was no pain, but she knew it was Asher. Turning to look at him, she could see that he'd been burned too and started to pull away.

"No. Not yet. I just need to hold you." Essie nodded again, feeling out of sorts when she looked at Kiaran. He was a dragon now, and he looked like he might have taken some damage as well.

Essie pulled from Asher again, and he let her. Turning to the door, she wasn't really surprised to see that not only was there no door left, but some of the cabinets had been scorched as well. Essie looked at the dragon.

"You didn't have to do that. I was leaving anyway. Hurting the people who live here and this lovely house wasn't necessary. As I said, I was—"

You think I did this? He was still a dragon, but she could understand him. She wasn't sure how, but she nodded at him anyway. *You think that I'd burn my friend, my host, to get at you? You think...Christ, you do. You think I did this to you. Doesn't the fact that I saved you mean a thing to you?*

"You're not allowed to be all pissy with me, buster." She moved toward him and poked him in the chest with her hand as she spoke to him. "You're the one that told me I wasn't good enough for him. Accused me of bedding him to get...I fucking have no idea, but you are not going to get mad at me when I'm in a fine pissed off mood myself."

I can see that. She turned and glared at Asher when Kiaran moved toward him and disappeared. She knew that the dragon lived on Asher's body, but to see it sort of melt into him made her dizzy. When Asher reached for her, she smacked his hand away.

"He was protecting me." She nodded and backed from him. "I want to touch you again. I need to know that you're all right."

"I'm just fine and dandy. And I'll be better when I'm out of here." Asher shook his head. "Oh yes, I am going. This place and all of you are fruity."

His laughter caught her off guard, and she nearly fell back when he reached for her again. Essie thought his laughter was the most beautiful sound she'd ever heard. Then she shook her head. She was not fanciful and that was what that sounded like to her.

"Kiaran said to tell you he's sorry." Nodding, she turned her back to Asher. "Essie, look at me please."

"I'm leaving. And tell him...I don't care what you tell him." His hands touched her shoulders, and she wanted to lean back into him. "I didn't come here to seduce you. I was just fine where I was."

His mouth moved along the back of her neck to her shoulder. She felt his hands slide down her arms to her waist, and he pulled her back to his chest. Her body felt like he'd stroked her, not just where he was touching her but everywhere, inside and out.

"The burn on your body, it was caused by the same witch that touched you. I can smell it on you." She stiffened and started to turn when he held her still. "No, listen to me. The fact that you were burned by her makes me think that she knows what we are. Not the family but what you are to me."

"I'm nothing to you, Asher. We had sex, that's it." His hot breath on her bare shoulder made her shiver. "Stop that. I can't think when you're breathing all over me. I have to get out of here before I let you fuck me again."

"I'm okay with that." She growled at him and felt something move along her skin. "It's Kiaran. He's got it in his head that you hate him. I can understand why you're mad at him. He told me what he said to you. But he's very sorry."

"I don't hate anyone. It's a waste of time and energy. But he did hurt me." The movement along her skin made her think of the dragon tat on Asher's body. "He said you were his host. What does that mean?"

He pulled back from her, and she felt the loss of the heat immediately. But when he took her hand and led her to the table and asked her to sit, she realized that it was just the two of them in this room. Or three. She wasn't sure what to do with Kiaran.

"When...I'm not really sure where to start. Okay...." He sat down. "I'm nearly three thousand years old."

She wanted him to say he was kidding but just knew that he wasn't. Getting up, she went to the cabinet and pulled down a glass. She'd been in the house enough over the last few weeks, coming in to shower and stuff, that she'd been able to find where everything was stored. After getting a glass of water with ice, she sat back down, her mind not even considering what he'd just said as anything but the truth.

"Let's just say that you are three thousand years old and that I'm going to believe you." He nodded. "What does all of this mean? And I think you need to explain to me the part that you have a dragon that lives on your body and he's not you at all." Even to her own ears that made absolutely no sense, but Asher seemed to understand her.

"Long ago, before I was born, my mother and father lived in the village near a castle. The king, Anthony, was a good king by all accounts. His wife the same. She was adored by her people as much as her husband. But they were dragons." Essie nodded. "One day, right after a big storm came through the village and knocked over buildings and ruined crops, Anthony and Eve were flying over to see the damage. It was probably not the smartest thing to do with tempers high over the damage that had been caused. And so far as I know, this was something that they did a lot…surveying the land for things out of order and to see if anyone was struggling with their crops or farm. As I said, they were very good to their subjects and were only looking out for them."

"This would be Kiaran's parents, I'm betting." He told her it was. "And somehow, people being what they are, they blamed everything on the dragons. I don't suppose anyone thought to ask them what they were doing out there, did they?"

"No. It wasn't…I think someone might have gotten them worked up about things when it was just as easy for it to be put to rest. But you're right, they were Kiaran's parents. The king and queen had six sons. Eve had just given birth to six hatchlings a few weeks before. She'd hidden them away, deep in the mountain, just before they were out where the people could see them. The people, most of them, attacked the couple, and Eve gave her life protecting her young. Anthony was hurt badly in the process, but knew that he'd have to do something quickly to save his children."

Essie could almost see it taking place. The dragon queen, trying to save her children and killing a great many people before she'd been killed herself. And her spouse, a man who more than likely loved his wife more than his own life, did something that no human man would do…put his children's lives ahead of his own.

"He brought my father to him that night, a man he thought of a great deal, and my mother as well. They'd never met before then, and he told them what he needed them to do. He said that they'd have six sons, and sometime after they were born, his son's would come to them as babes and protect them. We would protect each other." Essie nodded, almost afraid for him to continue. "A few days after I was born, Kiaran came to me. Wrapped his body around mine and stayed with me. Forever. And so long as one of us lives, the other will as well. My brothers have the same duty as I do. To protect them with our lives, as they would us."

Essie sat there for several minutes. He never spoke again, for which she was grateful. She wanted to tell him her story, tell him that she was a hunted person, but only stood up and went to the opening where the door had once been. Before stepping out, she turned to him.

"I know the witch. She's my mother. She doesn't...I think she no longer has any idea who I am. I've been gone from her a very long time. When she hurt me the other day, it was because I was in the wrong place at the wrong time. She'd been startled, as was I, and she attacked." She looked down at the wrap that held some vile-smelling medicine before continuing. "I'd like for you to leave me alone now. I don't know...she more than likely won't come after me again. It was like I said, a one-time thing. But she's not a nice person, and I don't want to be responsible for her harming anyone here. Especially Mr. Jacob or Elbert."

She left them, his laughter ringing out the door after her. Essie liked the sound and was afraid she'd get used to hearing it, only to be tossed away again. No, this was better, she thought, to get away now before she became too attached to him.

Chapter 4

Asher didn't go after her. But he did ask the earth around him to keep her safe and to alert him when she was in danger. His duty now was to keep her as safe as he would Kiaran. Calling the dragon out, he watched as the man paced the room.

"I hurt her. Badly, I think. And not just her feelings, but her body as well. I didn't get to heal her burns completely." Asher said nothing as Kiaran continued. "I only wanted to see if the witch had sent her here to find us. The cut on her arm...I don't think it was put there on purpose, but I missed why in her memories."

"She fought with the witch. Tore into her when she came upon her when she was stealing herbs from the forest beyond our home. The herbs are those of another tenant on the land, and the old woman that lives there was very upset that the witch was taking them from her. Essie stepped in and fought her for them. She is the witch's daughter, in case you missed that. She just told me that part. Neither of them have seen each other for a long time, and Essie is pretty sure that the witch has no idea who or what she is to her. And Essie has something that her mother wants from her —

or so she believes." Kiaran asked him how he knew that. "I was with her when she rested, remember? Her dreams are full of nightmares that you and I would think horrific. And we both know how much we've seen."

Kiaran nodded before talking again. "What is it she thinks that Essie has? I mean, I've been to her home, where she's been staying, several times. There is nothing there of any value."

"You know as well as I do that one person's value could be nothing to everyone else." Kiaran nodded. "You have to fix this with her. You know that she's my wife now, according to our laws and morals. And I can't have the two of you at odds any more than you can."

"She...I will admit I thought her not good enough for you. No. That's not right. I didn't want her to be good enough for you." Kiaran stopped pacing and looked at him. "Asher, she has something that no other woman I've met has. Did you know that?"

Asher nodded. He didn't know what it was she had, but he knew there was something extraordinary about her. Asher thought of all the things he'd learned about her, and some of the things that he wished he knew now.

"She sees Dad." Kiaran told him that she talked to him through their link as well. "See, more things to add to our list of things that she can do. I can taste some magic on her...not a lot, I don't think, unless she's hiding it from me. Which, I suppose, is possible. But there's more to her than we can see on the surface."

"Her body was burned badly. Had I not been here...." Kiaran shivered. "I promise I'll make this right between the two of us. And see if I can get her to come back here. I've never seen you so...I was going to say laid back, but I think it's just because you've been laid."

Asher picked up the sponge that was on the table and tossed it at his other half. Because after years and years of not understanding what they were to each other, they had figured out that being a part of something whole was the best way to explain it to themselves. Kiaran left a few minutes later, going out into the yard.

Standing up, Asher surveyed the damage done to the doorway. Lifting his hands up, he placed them on either side of the opening. Closing his eyes, he used some of the gifts that his mother had given him when she bore him. Magic coursed through his body much like his blood, making him a very strong and extremely dangerous person. The entire area was instantly back to the way it had been before the heat blasted into the room.

With the damage fixed, he realized he'd gotten something else. Something that he'd never gotten from repairing damage before—a connection to the person who had done this. The witch was indeed trying to kill Essie, and the reason why surprised him more than the knowledge that she'd done it. Essie wasn't just her daughter but something more…much more than anyone might know. And she was strong too. Very much so.

"What do you see, son?" Asher turned slowly to look at his father. His father had been gone from Asher's life longer than he was in it…it had been that long since he'd seen his father. And the joy he felt that he'd come to him now was nearly too much for him. Asher stared in disbelief at the man before him. "It's me. You're not going to have a fit, are you? That I've been around for a while?"

"No. I knew you were." His dad nodded. "Where's Mom? Why is she not here with you? I'm assuming that she knows that you're here."

"She does, but she can't come. Not that she doesn't want to, but she can't. She's not...I want to tell you something. Something that I should have told you a long time ago. All of you." Asher nodded and leaned against the counter to listen. "The girl? What do you think of her? Something else, isn't she?"

"Yes. I'm assuming that you thought she'd be my wife?" His dad nodded. "What if I didn't want her? Or anyone in my life. What would you have done then?"

"You need someone in your life, Asher. You were never meant to be alone. None of you were." Asher didn't say anything as his father continued. "Elbert said that you and...that the two of you are man and wife now. I'm glad for that."

"She's left me again." His dad looked out the door and beyond to the mountain. "Yes, that's where she's gone. She and Kiaran had words and she's pissed at him. And at me, I suppose. You should have stayed out of it."

"I should have. But I didn't. And I won't now." Asher asked him what he had to tell him. "I'm working up to it. I'm not as quick on the mark as you and the other boys are. I need to work it out."

"Her mother is looking for her. She thinks that Essie is more powerful than her. I think she might be right. But what does killing Essie do to make her any stronger?" His dad sat down and didn't answer him. "Dad, I can't help her if you don't tell me everything."

"She's been to the tomb. Essie has. She's been there a lot. It's in her cave." Asher sat as well. No one, so far as he knew, had ever been there. There was no one beyond his family who even knew it existed. "The queen...I think the queen passed something on to her that even Essie is not aware of yet. I can see it on her."

"But the witch knows, doesn't she? Knows that the dead queen, after thousands of years, has given something — we don't know what — to a woman that is my wife. Great. Is there anything else that I should know?" His dad nodded. "And what happens to it if Essie is dead? Does it go to her mother?"

"Not necessarily. It goes to the person who takes her life." Asher had known that but didn't want to think on it. "Kiaran and her, Essie, they have a connection as well."

"He told me just now." His dad nodded and got up to pace. "What else, Dad? Should I call the rest of them here? Just to keep her safe? Because as much as I'd like to take her to them, I'm thinking there is more magic here to help us than at home."

"Essie has her own magic, as you already know. I was with her a few days before her mother found her, and could see her glowing with it. She didn't know, of course, that she has something more. And so you know, Helena has no idea who she is other than she has magic that she wants. I don't think Essie would tell anyone about any of you. But she's been touched by the same magic I received when I saw the king that night." Asher could remember the stories that his parents had told them over and over, and how he'd gotten his name; Asher for the ash of the kingdom, and Anthony, who brought his parents together.

"How is that even possible? The dead are that, Dad…dead." His dad stopped pacing and looked at him with a cocked brow. "Good point. You're here, aren't you? But I don't understand what could have been given to her. Or did she simply take it?"

"I don't know. And I've not asked. But she needs to take you to the tomb. You and she need to go there with Kiaran." He asked him why. "The day your brothers were born, their dragons came to them. Immediately. There wasn't a delay like there was with you. A near week had gone by without him coming to you, and we feared for your life. You'd not nurse, and you cried until you were weak with it. I had thought that the hatchling had been injured somehow, and that the death of the egg would mean that you were going to die as well."

"But he came." His dad nodded. "Then what? Everything was okay? You never found out what happened?"

"No. I asked Kiaran about it. He just looked confused. I don't think he knows what happened either. And like I told you, the rest of his brothers came within minutes of my sons, your brothers, being born."

Asher knew that there was something else, maybe something that his dad did not know, and felt that he and Kiaran should investigate. He stood up to go and see the tomb with Essie and Kiaran.

"What are you going to do now?"

"Bring her back here. I know now that she's safer here. And so will the tomb be safe, I think, with her away from it. I'm hoping that I can get her to trust me enough that she shares whatever she knows with me. I think that — and this is just thinking — she is the key to this." His dad said that he agreed. "Dad, does she have magic that she'll share with me?"

His dad stood up and smiled. "Son, she has given you all that she is. And you have shared as well. It's why I thought...no, it's not what I thought when I had Elbert bring you here. I thought that you'd find someone that you could have some fun with. I hoped for love and marriage, but didn't expect it. Now I can see that I made a good choice."

Asher thought so too, but only nodded before telling his dad what he was going to need from him. "I'm calling the rest of them here. All of us together should be able to figure this out. And I want you to talk to them." His dad shook his head. "Dad, they have a right to know that you're around. We've really missed you."

"I've missed you as well. And I'll think on it. It's hard on me, you know. Staying here talking when I should be resting." Asher nodded. "I'll work on it. In the meantime, go and get the girl and bring her home. She needs you as much as you do her."

~~~

Essie was sitting next to her little fire when she felt the dragon. Her not turning to acknowledge him only made him laugh. Essie didn't want to smile at the way his laugh made her feel, so she kept her back to him.

"I came to make amends with you." She snorted at him and put her little pot over the flames to boil some water. Her one vice was tea, and she spent more on it than she should, being as broke and on the run as she was. But she loved it, and it was all she ever treated herself with. "I know that Elbert makes some very nice tea. I've drank it a few times when he's been in the mood to share it with me. He makes scones too. Strawberry ones."

She turned to look at him. Scones were her downfall. And she loved strawberries as much as she did her tea. But like a lot of things, she seldom could get them. Turning her back to him, she tried to think of a way to show him she didn't care.

"Mr. Kiaran, if Asher sent you here to make these amends, then you can shove those up your ass. I don't want anything from you. And in the event you didn't notice, I'm not near your precious Asher." His laughter had her turning to him again. He was sitting down now and he'd taken off the jacket he always wore. It startled her to see a dragon crest on his forearm. "You're marked."

He looked surprised that she could see it, and he pulled his sleeve up so that she could see it all. It looked like a crest of someone's and a dragon holding it in his claws. She stood to get a closer look. As she studied it, he turned his forearm to and fro for her to get the entire picture. Yes, that's what it was, a lovely silver dragon that looked like it had just been made, and the silver was still very well preserved. And on the crest was a swirl of some sort that she'd bet was flames.

"I didn't have it put on here, if that's what you're thinking. I'm not sure, but I think it's from my father. I never met him, of course, but back then a crest was worn on everything. I wish I could have seen it. It would have been great to see, but since the castle was burned to the ground, there would have been nothing left of those either." He pulled the sleeve down. "My brothers don't have a mark. None of them. I think perhaps it's because I'm the oldest."

She didn't think so and asked him if she could touch it. He hesitated, and she started to go back to her fire when he put out his arm. The sleeve was pulled back up, and she thought maybe she shouldn't be doing this.

"It might hurt. It...the only other time I've done this, the person was bad, I guess you could say, and it hurt him." He asked her if she would be hurt. "Yes. But not like you might be."

"Then I would rather you didn't do it. I think I've hurt you enough."

He started to pull the shirt back over it, but she put her hand on the marking. The pain was there, but it wasn't nearly as bad as she'd expected.

"It's not from your father, but your mom. She wanted you to have something of his and she gave you this. It's power. You need only to ask for it and it will be yours." Kiaran asked her what that meant. "I don't know. But she seemed to think that you'd know when the time was right. Also...."

Essie pulled her hand away and looked at the opening of her cave. Asher stood there, looking like he knew a great secret. Instead of telling Kiaran what else she'd found, she got up and went to the back of her cave.

"I have something to show you both. I have to show you, not that I want to." Kiaran asked her what the difference was. "I love the place deep within the cave, and when I visit there, I feel like I'm a part of something huge. It's a tomb I think. Where your mother is."

"You're going to take us there?" She nodded at Asher's question and turned to look at them both when he said her name. "I wasn't going to ask you, but I think it's important."

"You've been there a lot, to the tomb?" Essie nodded at Kiaran's question. "Thank you for this then. I wanted to go and see it, but I had no idea where it was."

Kiaran stood up and looked at them both. Essie wasn't sure if this was a good idea or not, but it was beyond her control now. The sigil on Kiaran's arm had told her what she was to do.

She was going down the long path that she'd cleared as she spoke. She told herself she was going to get this over with. It was why she didn't look at them, but the truth was, she didn't want to see the disbelief or even fear on their faces when she told them.

"Your mother knew I would come into your lives. She even knew my name. Of course, she called me Esmerelda, but I guess nicknames weren't all that common back then. Anyway, she said that I was to take you there and that you'd understand." Asher asked her what they would understand. "I have no idea. Just that you would. She warned that I shouldn't touch anything."

"But it's too late for that, isn't it, Essie?" She nodded and realized that they might not see her in the darkened tunnel they were currently in, and told Asher yes. "What did you touch? Whatever it is, my dad said that you got something from it. Magical, he said."

"It knocked me on my ass. Then when I woke up, I could see things. Not with my eyes, but by touching them. I could do that before, somewhat, but not like now. It's like I have a connection to everything I can feel."

Asher said nothing, and neither did Kiaran.

The air down here was dank, not nasty like she'd expected, but the smell of old and maybe a little wet. She'd noticed too that the closer that she'd gotten to the large chamber, the more it smelled of a female. A very expensive female that liked very nice perfume.

As they made their way down, Asher stepped in front of her. He never took over leading them, but he did go first through the rest of the tunnels, as well as helped her over the larger stones that she'd been unable to move. Twice Kiaran helped her when she started to slide back on the somewhat slick path, but he never got in front of her like he, too, would take over. It was like they were protecting her or something, which was strange to her since she was pretty sure neither of them cared all that much for her.

As soon as they were at the opening of the chamber, she stopped them. Essie was sort of afraid to take them in. Not that they'd bother anything within, but she didn't want them to discard her just yet. She knew that once they found the chamber, they'd no longer have any use for her.

"I'll just go on up now." Asher took her hand when she turned. "You no longer need me to show you where it's at. Just go beyond this small opening and to the left. Not like you can go right, but it's right there."

"I want you to be with me. We both do." Kiaran nodded and took her other hand. "Come with us. Show us what you found for us. I'm sure that we're going to…Essie, I want you with me when I go there. I need you with me."

"As do I." She started to shake her head no to Kiaran, to tell him — well, them — that they were big bad assed men and she wasn't, but they pulled her along with them until they were in the room. "Holy shit," Kiaran said, and she had to agree with him.

The room was the largest place she'd ever been in inside of the caves. Actually, it was larger than most houses she'd been in as well. The walls were solid stone that reached to the top at about two hundred feet. The floor, even covered in broken stones and sand, was wider and longer than a football field twice over. There was light here, however, shining seemingly from every corner of the place.

Essie had found the source of the light the second time she'd come down here. At least a little of the light that was needed to brighten the room. Diamonds and other gems lined the walls, the light reflecting off them until it made a beautiful pattern on the floor that changed with each passing hour. Even at night — because she'd stayed once to see — it was as bright as the fire that she cooked with.

Both men stood in the opening, not moving beyond the door. She did, however, and moved to the six broken eggs that were there. The first time she'd been here, it had taken her a bit to figure out what they were. But it was the skeletal remains of the woman that had taken her breath away.

"I didn't know what had happened at first. I found her just like she is, laying outstretched as if she were pointing to them, her other hand holding onto the first one like she wanted to pull it to her. Then after talking to Mr. Jacob, I realized what she was. The dragon queen. And she's not pointing, but protecting." Kiaran came closer to the body but didn't touch her. "She's laying over the first egg. It's as if she were covering it with her wing when she died. I would imagine that when you were born, you had difficulty getting out from under her. She would have been a dragon still."

"She would have been. Her form wouldn't have gone back to human until much later." Asher said nothing as Kiaran continued. "My father and she thought that they were the last of their kind, I think. They must have been a sight to see flying together over the fields and mountains."

"You said that she told you to bring us here." Essie nodded at Asher, who still had not come completely into the room. "Do you know why? Or is seeing where she lay what we needed to understand? My father just told me of how Kiaran came to me. I can tell him now why it took him a week. He had to...it must have been hard to come from under her."

"I don't remember." Kiaran stood up and moved to where his mother's hand was over his long forgotten shell. "She was marking me, I think. Putting this on my arm so that you could find me."

"I don't know." Essie stood up and moved to the other side of the room. "But this is what I need to show you. I haven't seen it myself, but I know that something is here."

The key was just where Eve had told her it would be. Lifting the stone up was easier than she'd thought it would be, and she picked the large key out of the broken stone. Before she put it in the opening that was hidden behind another stone, she turned and looked at Asher.

"She had a message for you as well." Asher nodded and finally moved into the room. "The riches beyond are yours to use. Use them, she asks, to rebuild what was once theirs, what was once yours."

"She wants me to rebuild the castle?" Essie told him she didn't know. But she had a feeling that that was what she wanted. "I can do that now, Essie. I don't need whatever is on the other side of the wall. Whatever is in there is Kiaran's and the other dragons', not mine."

"Maybe so, but she said it is yours." She twisted the key in the lock. It turned easily, the clicking of the lock loud in the chamber that was so large. When the door started to move, sliding back on unseen hinges, she took a step back and bumped into Asher. He held her to him as the door opened completely.

"Oh my God." Asher held her as Kiaran walked around her. Even as the room brightened little by little, the stones on the walls capturing as much light as they could, she could see that the room was filled with more than just monetary riches, but things that would mean so much more to all of them.

Chapter 5

Helena was standing over her book when she stilled. Something was wrong. Terribly wrong, and she had to sit down or fall as the wrongness of it took her breath away. The word Esmerelda touched her mind, and she felt the hatred of her daughter's blood as if she were standing before her right now.

The book she'd been working in was forgotten as she tried to concentrate on what had disturbed her. At one time she'd been able to reach into the earth, ask it for information, but since those people had come, she'd not had any luck with it. Not that she was ever going to give back what she took from them, but they were too stupid to know that. Now she knew that the man and his servant were the cause of her crisis.

Nothing answered her—not the stones on the ground or beneath it—nor did the trees sing their information to her. It was as if she'd been cut off from everything she needed. Going out of her home, she stood still, listening for anything that might help her. It wasn't until she stood there for several minutes that she realized that there were no sounds; not even the crickets were chirping.

The shadow that covered the ground seemed to grow as it came toward her. Backing up, she hit the wall behind her rather than going into the house as she'd planned. But before she could turn and get her bearings, the first of them flew over her head, and Helena covered her mouth so as not to scream.

There were five all together that darkened her sky, and each of them carried a man with them, caught hard in their claws. Fear like she'd never felt before settled over her. Not just over, she realized, but into her skin and bones. Even, she thought, into her blood. They were there for her to see. The dragons had returned.

When the sky no longer put them in her view, she hurried into her house and hid deep within the shadows. The fire in her house didn't remove the chill that the sight of the dragons had given her, and she doubted that she'd ever be warm again. They were back, her mind kept telling her, but her mind was still dealing with what it had yet to process. The dragons were back and they'd know.

Long ago, well before there were so many people in the world, Helena had been working in the castle. She'd been a cook for the king and queen, a job that she'd detested almost as much as she did them. But it was the only way she could get close enough to them to get what she needed. And still that prize had never been hers.

She'd not been there the day that the castle had fallen. Had she been then things for her would have been much different all these centuries later. Helena could have been the greatest witch in the world, but the storm had taken its toll and had ruined it all.

"I would have gotten their hearts but for that." She stood near her table again and looked at her notes. For centuries, even before the king had taken a wife, she'd been plotting to take the heart of the man who had the magic she desired. The magic that she deserved. Turning back the pages, far back almost to the beginning, she read her notes there.

"Heart of a dragon, oh so hot. The scale of a female, fertile and mine. The toe of a man, in love so strong. The hair of the woman who would be dead before long." She smiled at her rhyme, thinking herself quite clever even then. "Put them in a pot, stir them up hot. When the brew is done, all should be yours."

"Not the best rhyme, I suppose, but it was just a working spell." And it might have worked but for the fact that they'd both died in the flames that had consumed all that had been inside the castle when it fell. All but the scale that she'd found one day, which she'd snatched up before anyone could see it.

Helena went to her hearth and pulled the loose stone. With a quick look around, she reached into the hole and pulled out the leather bag and laid it upon the table. Wiping off the collection of spiders that had dared to be near her things, she dumped the contents of the bag on the book and stared at it.

The scale was perhaps as large as her book at about a foot long. The width of it was only about half that, but it was a nice one. From the belly, she thought. Helena didn't touch the scale this time but poked at it with a stick. The last time she'd been stupid enough to touch it, twenty-some years ago, she'd ended up with her daughter. The fertility spell was very powerful.

"A heart. All I need is a heart and a couple of humans and I can take what is mine." Helena didn't know what it was that she wanted. It changed from day to day. To be honest, she thought, perhaps it changed more than that, whenever she saw a new bauble or something shiny. It was why she was living where she was. All her money would be gone as soon as she made it.

The knock at the door had her leaping from it in fear, and a small whimper left her mouth.

The house that she lived in was not much more than a lean-to. There were walls, of course, on all four sides, two of them buried deeply within the mountain that she gathered her herbs from. There was only the one room, with a hearth that she used daily for her brews or magic and a cot, which was nothing more than a tick mattress lying on a stack of hay bales. She'd had more—a bigger house, of course—but that had taken more magic to keep up than her appearance. And she needed her looks like she did her breath.

"Miss Helena? I've come for the potion you said you'd make for me. It's Judy Wade. Do you remember me?" Helena rolled her eyes. She remembered the homely girl. "You told me to come back today. I have the money."

Helena asked her to wait. Scooping up the scale with a stick and spoon, she put it back in its hiding place and went to answer the door. Helena changed her appearance just enough so that the woman would never recognize her if she saw her again. She opened the door.

"I have the money you said you'd need." Helena nodded and took the cash. It was stolen from Judy's neighbor and from her husband's wallet. Not that Helena cared where the money came from, but it was nice to know that the woman would go to such risks to get what she wanted. A woman after her own heart, she thought. If not for the fact that she was stupid.

"I want to have a child with my husband, like I told you." Helena nodded and asked her to have a seat. To be honest, she'd forgotten to make her something up and now had to think what she might have on hand to pretend with. "I was hoping for a new baby for Christmas. Do you think I'll be able to make an announcement by then?"

It was four or five months away, but Helena doubted that if she had years before the requested date that she'd ever make it. Judy's husband had been snipped and burned. There would be no child from his body. Picking up the spoon she'd used to push the scale into the bag, she had a sudden thought.

"I need for you to trust me on this." Judy nodded, looking at her as if she thought her a goddess. Well, right now she felt like one. "I want you to hold this spoon in your mouth for five minutes. Then you have to go home and fuck your husband."

The woman looked shocked but eager. Helena handed her the spoon, only to snatch it back at the last second. She didn't want her coming back when it didn't work. Capturing her eyes in her own gaze, she pulled the woman under her spell. "See a man, fuck him good. Ride his cock hard and quick. When he comes, suck him off. Then take him back to fuck again."

When the woman blinked at her several times, Helena handed over the spoon. It was in her head to say some words over the woman, just to make it look good, but the spoon popped in her mouth as if it were attached to her there.

As she left, Helena thought of asking her to return the spoon, as she only had two more, but instead told the woman never to return.

"It will work or it will not. But know this; if you return here to my home, all that is yours will be mine, and I will kill any issue that you have as well. And you should know that any man you fuck will fill your belly with a babe."

Judy's eyes brightened, and Helena nearly asked her who she was thinking about but didn't. "Go, and as I have warned you, never return."

Returning to her book, she sat down. There was only so much she could do with her book right now, but the money in her hand made her think of all the things she could get to help with other spells. Like the one to kill her daughter.

"Elsie, or whatever you call yourself, you are going to die if you aren't close to it already." Helena thought of the girl she'd seen a few days ago. The nerve of the chit to yell at her like she was nothing more than a common person. "If you were a daughter of mine, I would have ripped your heart out and boiled it for my supper." She never would. Eating a heart was for trolls and other creatures, not for Helena, the blackest witch of all time.

When she'd tried to burn the girl days later at the house by tossing her magic at the door, Helena had failed at that as well. Her magic was very powerful, but only when it touched the person. Helena had followed her scent that day, all the way to the house. It had surprised her when the creature had leapt to save her. Helena would have sworn it was a dragon from the brief glimpse she had of it, but she knew they were all dead. The way it had wrapped around her, keeping her from the worst of her magic, had been heartbreaking to Helena. But she'd find out soon enough. Both the man and the woman would die before it got around that she was a failure at magic. That just would not do. It was hard enough finding work when there was so little call for a witch nowadays.

~~~

Asher hugged his brothers. He'd never been so glad to see them in his entire life. But he also had so much to tell them, more than any of them would believe. But first things first, he had to find Essie.

Jed sat at the table now, groaning from the amount of food he'd eaten. Elbert must have made several trips to town to bring in even a part of what he'd cooked. Christ, it looked like he was feeding several hungry troops gone to war. But the dragons were joining them tonight, and they were a hungry lot even on the best of days.

His brother asked him what he was looking for when he got up to look in the kitchen again. "Whatever it is, I'm sure that it can wait until you tell us why you summoned us here. Not that I'm not thrilled to be here, but we left work undone and some things that needed taken care of for you."

"I have news." Shane laughed when Asher sat down, but then quickly stood up again as he tried to explain. "I have a lot of news. Some of it is going to be hard to believe, but I can tell you, it's all true."

When all of them stood up, dropping whatever they had in their hands and staring at the doorway behind him, Asher turned as well, smiling. He knew that she'd come to him, and was glad to see her. Taking her hand, he pulled her along with him as he stood closer to the head of the table.

"Everyone, this is Esmerelda Hahn Benson, my wife." She slapped him and tried to pull away, but he held her firmly. "She's still getting used to the idea of being married to me."

"Christ, man." Gideon put out his hand to touch her, and Essie moved back. "Just wanting to know if you're real or not, love. I've never seen a more beautiful creature in my life."

Asher felt her embarrassment and asked them all to have a seat. Jed kept standing and once they were all seated, he came toward her and bowed. Essie looked at Asher, then at Jed again.

"My lady, sister. I welcome you to this family." Jed stood and took her hand. As he kissed it on her palm, Asher realized what he was doing. He was getting her taste, and he was glad that someone had thought of that. "I am Jedidiah Benson, second son to Jacob and Sally Benson. My dragon is Zak, also second son, but to the King Anthony and his wife Queen Eve."

Elam stood next and kissed her palm, but Asher noticed that it wasn't in the same spot where Jed had kissed her. "I am Elam Benson, third son to Jacob and Sally Benson. My dragon is Casdon, also third son but to the King Anthony and his wife Queen Eve, and the best friend of myself."

When Shane stood up, Essie put her hand up. "I get that you're all the sons of Jacob and Sally Benson. And if you stay in order, I'll get that too. But if you introduce yourself so formally, we're going to be here a long time." Shane laughed and kissed her hand. "That's not necessary either. You don't have to kiss me just because Asher thinks we're married."

"Ah my dear, but we do have to kiss a part of you. And your hand is much safer for us all than anywhere else on your pretty body." Shane winked at her as he kissed her other palm. "We are taking in your taste, my dear, so that we can find you no matter what. Our magic from our mother gives us the ability to do a great many things that will keep you safe. And my dragon is Keion."

Gideon stood as well, and as if she'd not asked him to keep it simple, he told her his name and his parents' names, as well as that of his dragon Onimia. But instead of kissing her palm, he took her into his arms and dipped her back, kissing her soundly on the mouth, much to the amusement of everyone but Asher. He would make Gideon pay for that later.

Simeon was last, and he didn't kiss her palm but put his nose into her throat. No one said anything as he pulled back and licked his lips. Asher was afraid that he'd bitten her; the magic that was his and his alone would require him to do so. It wasn't until he sat down that he noticed the drop of blood on his lip. Asher wanted to ask him what he'd found but didn't. This was not the time.

"I'm so happy to meet you all." Essie moved to the window before she continued. "I've heard so much about you. Your powers and magic. I wasn't told why I was supposed to live here, but when your brother showed up, Mr. Jacob finally told me."

"Mr. Who?" Asher started to explain but Elbert came in. He was holding a large platter of ham and was hurriedly helped to place it in the center of the table. Elam asked again who Essie was talking about.

"Me. She's talking about me." No one said a word when their dad came into the room. He was just suddenly there, and he walked over to Essie and stood by her. "She's my friend, and when I saw her here a few months ago, I thought she'd be perfect for Asher."

"Dad?" Simeon was the first to speak, and when their dad nodded at him, he stood up. "Mom? Is Mom here too? I...can we see her too?"

"No. I don't know what the problem is with her coming to talk to you. I can see her on the other side, talk to her some, but not well. She is trying to tell me something, but I've yet to figure it out. But I am glad to see the lot of you."

Each of the dragons welcomed their dad in much the same way as his brothers did, telling him they were glad he was around and asking after his wife. Their mother had raised the dragons as much as she had the boys. Sally Benson had been a good woman, and the best mom a boy to man could have ever asked for.

It wasn't as if none of them had seen a woman before, but Asher had never seen them look so uncomfortable as they did around Essie. She wasn't helping matters by being slightly standoffish. Asher was sure it was because she was overwhelmed. To have fourteen men in the same room, all of them tripping over themselves not to offend her, was almost too funny. Then she put her fingers into her mouth and let out a shrill whistle that made them all grow silent.

"I'm a woman, not a girl. I can curse better than you guys can; I can drink a six pack of beer right along with the best of men. I carry a knife when I can afford one. I've been in a lot of bar fights, and I'm pretty sure that I can play a good game of chess. Not perfect, but pretty good." She looked at Asher before continuing to address the rest of them. "The next one of you that tells me you're sorry for your language, the fact that you think you might have said the wrong thing, or just generally acting like you're not from this century, I will knock you on your asses and stomp it while I'm at it. Clear?"

Apparently they all got it, because before dinner was completely on the table, it was as if she were a part of the family and she'd been dining with them since they were kids. Asher fell right over his head in love with her right then and there.

Dinner, as it usually was when they were all together, was loud and full of laughter. Asher kept an eye on Essie, but she seemed to be holding her own. He watched her take

Elam to task about something he said, and then she'd hugged Shane tightly when he looked like he was going to leave the table. As they helped clear the table, setting up the dishwasher for it to start, she was right there with them, helping them with that as well.

"We have more to tell you." Kiaran sat next to him and pulled out the pouch that had been part of what they'd discovered. "We went to the resting place of our mom today. And this...this is why we called you all here."

As Kiaran dumped the pouch on the table, no one said a word. Asher wasn't sure if they were stunned by the fact that they'd gone to the tomb or by the items on the table. Either one would have rendered the stoutest of men silent.

"Are those...are those the king and queen?" The small pendants were picked up by Simeon, who held them with reverence. "I've never seen anything so detailed before. And look how much Kiaran looks like his father."

They were passed around to each of them. Asher had seen them and helped Elbert bring in the bottles of wine and the glasses they'd need. When he returned, Essie was telling them how she'd found the tomb.

"I was hiding out in the caves. My mother had been close to where I was staying once or twice, and I was going to see if I could find me a back door out. I moved down deeper into the cave, and was intrigued that instead of getting darker, it seemed to get brighter with each step I took. By the time I made it to the bottom, I was afraid that I'd be trapped." Asher handed her a glass of wine, and she pushed it away. He'd have to remember that. She didn't drink at all. "I saw her first... the woman's body. And the only reason I knew that it was female because of the clothing she had over her. Then I saw the eggs."

"Six of them." She nodded at Casdon. "I don't remember the place. Isn't that strange? We all spent time there, living and waiting for our other half to be born, and I can't remember a thing about the place."

"I was asked recently why it took me so long to come to Asher. I had no idea until today." Kiaran looked at Asher's dad as he explained. "She was laying over me. Her hand was curled around my shell as if she were pulling me to her. I think that's when she marked me. Gave me something to use. It wasn't until Essie touched it that I was told that it was indeed a sigil and not a remembrance from our father, like I had thought. And she knew that Essie here was coming to help me find these things."

Along with the pendants, there were jewels. Not a great many of them compared to what was in the locked away room, but enough for them to see the quality of gems that were hidden away. Asher told them of the scrolls that were there. Of the large crates of coins. The gold that lay in large bricks, row after row. He told them of the winged creatures that had been sculpted and of the armor that was there as well.

"You think they were hoarding it?" Asher shook his head at Gideon's question. "Then what? From what Dad told us there was plenty of money for the village. Whenever anyone needed anything it was there for them. But this room, it sounds like it had more than even the little village could have held."

"Don't you understand?" They all looked at Essie when she spoke. "They were dragons that had been here for longer than you guys. You can't think that they were born only hours before you were conceived, do you? You don't think that they only became king and queen of the village after only a few short years on this earth? They amassed this fortune from lifetimes. Maybe thousands and thousands of years before anyone even knew that they were around. They were saving for their children."

When no one said anything, she stood up and pulled the largest item from the pouch. Asher had had no idea that it was in the bag, but looked at it now when she gave it to him. He looked at his dad, then back at the framed picture that had been painted by a good hand, showing it to Jacob before he asked for it. His dad sat down and stared at it before he finally spoke.

"It looks like your mother." Asher nodded. "I mean, it could be her twin. You think he knew our families? You think…you think he brought us together because of our family ties?"

"I do." Essie took the framed painting from him and sat it on the table. "I believe that your family and that of the king and queen had been linked for more years than anyone will ever know. They were friends, and that was how he knew that he could trust you with such an undertaking. He knew that you'd watch over his children as well as he would."

Chapter 6

Essie didn't have a clue where she was supposed to go. The others were headed to the upper levels of the house, and she thought about going back to the cave. But after today she wanted to be in Asher's bed more than she wanted to be in the cold cave. How to get there was the problem.

When he came into the kitchen where she was, he leaned against the doorway. He was sexy as hell when he did that, and she was pretty sure he knew it. Crooking his finger at her, she nearly walked to him but shook her head. He grinned when she picked up a pan from the drainer when he came toward her.

"You wait right there." He stopped, but she had a feeling it wasn't because he was afraid of her, but more than likely humoring her. "You told them I was your wife. We are not married. I think I would have remembered that."

"According to my family law, and it dates back longer than you've been alive, once a man lays with a woman, they are wed." Frowning, she wondered what the hell that was supposed to mean. "My parents were laying on my father's shirt all night their first night together. He told me once that they talked about the stars and the moon, about the life of the king and queen, and the children that they'd have. He said that they even picked out names, trying their best not to think about the burning castle where their friend and king had been killed. She told him that she'd teach him to read, too, that night."

"So they didn't have sex, but since they shared a bed, no matter what kind, they were man and wife." He nodded as he took a few steps toward her and sat at the kitchen table. "That's not how it works now. There are vows to be said, rings exchanged, as well as some sort of license needs to be filled out and paid for. All the trappings that go with a wedding."

"Do you need all that?" His question caught her off guard, but before she could answer him, if she could think of one, he reached into his pants pocket and pulled out a tiny leather pouch. He slipped the string over his finger and let it hang there as he continued. "Kiaran gave this to me. He said that he'd asked his brothers first, and they all agreed that it was perfect. Each of them gave their blessing on our union."

"I don't need anything from you. But you can't go around telling people that we're married when we're not. It's…what if the right woman comes along and she believes that we're really married and you miss out?" He nodded again and came toward her, the pouch still hanging from his finger. "What are you doing?"

"I'm asking my wife to marry me." He dropped down on one knee in front of her. "I know that there are trappings, as you called them, that some people find themselves doing when they marry. Promises are made that are broken. Words are said that have no meaning. And love is bantered around like it's a ball in a court to be used against one another in pain as much as comfort. But I won't do that. I'll make you promises that I'll keep or won't give them. When I tell you that I love you, it's coming from my heart, not from my head. I will tell you how profoundly sorry I am if I hurt you, and you'll know that I mean it. I would never do a thing, not ever, to harm you either physically, verbally, or mentally."

He put the pouch on her finger like he'd had it on his own. It was heavier than she'd thought, and she wanted to open it to see what was there as much as she was afraid to. When she did nothing, he took it back from her and dumped it into his palm. When he slipped the heavy ring over her finger, all she could do was stare at it.

The beautiful, flawless diamond was on a wide white gold band. The gem was held onto the base by a pair of dragons, their mouths seemingly holding the diamond while their long tails made up a design around the gold. Their wings, spread wide, were almost too beautiful not to be thought of as real, forming a cover around the bottom of the diamond that kept it safe from beneath. It was a ring made for a queen.

"It's full of magic, this ring. Can you feel it?" She nodded and he smiled up at her. "Good. I was hoping that you would. Kiaran and the rest of them are magical, and have blessed the ring to keep you safe. Safe for me."

He stood up then and pulled her to him. His mouth was only a breath away from hers, and she wanted him to close the distance and kiss her. But he lifted his head and looked down at her this time. And waited.

"What?" Asher grinned. "You want me to tell you that I'll marry you? Or are you going to tell me this is a grand joke. That the moment that I think you're going to marry me they'll all come in here and laugh."

"So untrusting." He kissed her then and lifted his head again. "Say yes, Essie. Tell me you're going to be my wife, now and forever." At her nod he sealed his mouth over hers, and she felt it all the way to her toes and back up again. This time when he lifted his head, she was picked up in his arms and taken up the stairs. Essie knew that for the rest of the night, she was going to be well loved.

When he put her on her feet, she wasn't sure what to do, but he did. Moving behind her, he put his hands at her breasts and cupped them. When he pulled her body to his chest, she moaned when he began to toy with her nipples through her borrowed shirt, and put her hands over his.

"I'm going to strip you down slowly, kissing every part of you that I expose, and tasting you so that I can remember the flavor of you before I begin again." Her shirt was pulled over her head, and her nipples puckered tightly against the sudden chill. But he warmed them by rolling them in his large hands. "I'm going to eat you while you stand here. Drinking deeply of your pussy while I think of all the ways that I'm going to make you mine."

"Asher." He moaned when she reached behind her body and cupped his cock. He rocked into her as he nipped none too gently on her throat. "I want you. I want to feel you inside of me. Taking me slowly until I come over and over."

He slid his hand into the pants she had on and she nearly came when he touched her clit. As she rode his fingers, they slid in and out of her like she wished his cock was doing. Even as she got closer and closer to coming, he continued to fuck her from behind, his cock hard against her ass.

"Come for me. Come on my fingers so I can taste you."
She came hard, her body trembling with the release. Then
she watched, her body responding to his movements like he
was fucking her again, as he took his fingers to his mouth.
After he sucked them into his mouth, moaning at her taste,
he offered her his fingers as well and she licked them as he
had. When he came around her, holding her steady as he
did, she held his shoulders while he dropped to his knees.
"I'm going to enjoy this."

Before she could tell him she was as well, she was
naked for him. And when he pulled her to him by cupping
her ass, Essie nearly came again. His mouth sucked hard at
her nether lips, pulling them into his mouth even as he slid
his fingers inside of her. She rode his mouth as she had his
fingers, holding onto his head to keep him there. Not that
she thought he'd stop any time soon.

He ate her hungrily. Ravenously. Voraciously. She held
onto him, not to keep him to her but to keep from falling
now. His tongue, his fingers were touching her everywhere,
setting off tremors in their wake. And when he stood up,
his body covered in sweat, she cried out when he lifted her
up and slammed his cock deep inside of her, even as he
took her to the wall behind her.

"Come." She screamed out her release at his command.
And when he told her again, and again, she did that as
well. It seemed to not matter that she'd come several times
already; her body was ready for him each time he told her
to come. When he finally took her, his cum filling her,
touching her womb, Essie screamed again, her body bowed
up from the strength of her climax even as she slipped over
the edge of darkness and was swallowed up.

~~~

Asher put her to bed and covered her with the blankets that his mother had made for him so many years ago that he could no longer remember the year. But they smelled of her still. Her scent was in a lot of the things that he treasured here and at the house where they all lived in the city. Dressing again, weak with both the knowledge that he loved her and that she was his, he made his way to the lower levels to see Kiaran. He'd left him the moment they'd come upstairs.

"I'm so sorry." Kiaran asked him why. "I never thought of you having to be there when we had sex. I mean, I don't think of anything when she's with me, but I never thought of you and I being connected and what you must think of me."

"Honestly, I think of nothing. It's like when I'm resting. I go dormant when the two of you are in bed. But with everything going on, I decided that I'd come down here until...until...well, until it was safe." Kiaran laughed. "I take it she said yes."

"She did. Thank you for the ring. All of you. It is far better than what I would have chosen for her."

"My brothers want to go to the tomb tomorrow. But we didn't want to go without Essie. I think they think of her as some sort of keeper of our mother. I do too, as a matter of fact. She found her for us, and it's only fitting that she be there when the rest of us see her." Kiaran asked if he minded.

"No. But just so you know, with or without my permission, I'm pretty sure she'd go anyway." Kiaran nodded and laughed. "What have you found out about the witch? I know her name. It's Helena, no last name. And even Hahn is not Essie's real last name. I guess she gave it to herself when she was about six."

"I don't think her mother is young." Asher asked him what he meant. "I mean that she might be as old as, if not older than, us. When Essie told you it was her mother, I thought she was lying, but I've since changed my mind. I think that Essie is her daughter, but she had her very late in life. By magic. The same magic that flows through Essie."

"Magic?" Kiaran nodded. "Are you saying that she didn't inherit it from her parents, that it's as natural as...what? You and I? I know that she's powerful, and yet untapped in it. Why do you think this?"

"She lit the way to the chambers below ground with it. Essie said it was the gems, but the walls are too thick for any light to come through and make them shine. It's her. And when we entered the vault, it wasn't until she walked deeper in that the room was bright enough for us to see everything. I think she gets her powers the same way you do, from Mother Earth."

Asher thought about that as he made his way back up to his bed. He stood over her, staring down until he thought about holding her. Stripping down, he crawled into bed with her and was so glad that she rolled to him and wrapped around him. Asher closed his eyes thinking that he had to be the luckiest man on earth.

The dream—and it took him a few seconds to realize that it was a dream—was hers. He didn't know any of the people that were surrounding him, and he certainly had never thought about doing what they looked like they were about to do.

Looking around, he stared at the hooded people, if that's what they were. The hands holding the flowers, dead and dried out, were long, sharpened claws that were dark with age and blood. As he moved about the room, not tied to anyone or anything there, he noticed that the room was a large stone room, much like the one that they had entered just yesterday.

"You will not escape me this time, child of dragons. It is long past time that you gave me what I need." Turning to see into the circle of hooded people as they had moved to a sort of dais, what he saw there shocked him and scared him.

He was tied to the dais. But when he blinked several times, he could see that he'd been mistaken. It was his Essie there. Her arms and legs were outstretched in a way that it exposed everything. Her naked body had been covered in what appeared to him to be gold dust. She was looking around the room, but he could tell that she was drugged or something. As he pushed his way to her, Kiaran stopped him.

"It's a dream. Look around and see what you need to know. If this comes to pass, then we will need the advantage of having all this information." He nodded, but Asher wasn't so sure. Essie was tied up. "It's a dream, Asher. Remember that. It's just a dream."

When Kiaran was gone, he did as he was told. There were things here that made him think that this room had been used for this for centuries. But it was the woman in the black robe with white lilies on it that drew his attention.

Her hood was pulled over her head. The long robe dragged along the floor as she moved from one person to the next, the dust settling again and again on the hem. The flowers were real, sewn into the trim with red thread. The ribbons that hung from each flower stem were blood red as well. She had a long leather tie at her waist, and at the end of it was a pouch. He couldn't see what was in it, but the handle of what he thought was a blade was sticking out of the top.

The room was brightly lit by a fire that roared with life in a circle near the head of the dais. An entire wall held wood for it; enough, Asher was sure, to heat a house for several years. There were candles around too, but they did nothing to light the darkness in the corners where they were.

Someone walked to the fire, and Asher thought they were going to stoke it again, but instead they put something it in that flickered up shards of flames to the ceiling. It was then that he could see the markings up there.

He knew most of them…hieroglyphics that he'd seen on the walls of ancient caves; signs of worship of deities and other pagan gods. Asher read them twice, and reeled at the words and their meaning. When the flames died down to where he could no longer see the markings, he went back to the room in general.

There were two openings to the room. One had a large wooden door, the other nothing but a long silken sheet. He moved to that now and looked into the room beyond. Asher was stunned at what he saw.

There was a long table filled with food; not just plates of it, but large tubs filled with legs of lamb, hams…about a dozen of them…and baskets upon baskets of bread of different kinds. But it was the people at the table that shocked him. They were all dead, long dead.

The bodies were brittle, the skin long since gone. He walked up to one of them and could see that they wore jewels that were worth a fortune, and crowns marred by dust and webs. Age had darkened most of the gems, including the diamonds in the earrings of the women. Silken gowns and shirts that had long since rotted and started to fall apart held the bones together. The ties all but pulled apart from the strain of their weight. He was just reaching out to touch the crown of the man at the head of the table when he heard a scream. He knew it was Essie.

The blade sticking from her belly was shaking with her screams. Reaching her to pull it from her body, his fingers only passed through it. Her screams, louder now that he was near her, tore at him, his heart breaking with each one of them. The woman with the black robe stood over her; her voice, shrill in the stone room, demanded that Essie give it to her.

"Now, it is mine; they are all mine. Give it to me now. It belongs to me." Essie shook her head, tears streaming down her face as her mother commanded her to give it up. Then her mother plunged a second knife into Essie, stabbing her in the chest on the opposite side from her heart. "Give it to me."

"Never." The scream that came with the third knife entering her body had Asher falling to his knees, his body hurting with each of her wounds. When she turned to him, his Essie, he knew that she could see him, and he reached for her just as she spoke. "Never would I give you up. I love you."

Asher felt hands all over him. He fought them, using his fist, his feet, whatever he could to get away from them. There were voices too, someone screaming at him to wake up. Then the slap to his face had him opening his eyes.

"Christ." Jed was sitting on his chest and Gideon was holding onto his left arm, Simeon the other. There were others at his legs, but he was looking for Essie. Needed to see her. He looked at Jed when he said his name.

"Where is she? I need to see her." Jed nodded, then looked over at the window. She was there, but she wasn't awake. "Essie?"

"You hit her. It's what brought us to you. That and Kiaran. I've never seen him so afraid in my life. Christ, what the fuck were you dreaming about?" Struggling to sit up, he got up and went to her. Jed moved with him like he was afraid that he'd hit her again. Picking her up, he held her to his chest and asked what had happened.

"You were screaming, and when we came into the room with Kiaran, you were fighting against her. Essie was crying and you must have already hit her once, because there was blood on her mouth." Asher looked down at her face as Elam continued. "She turned to us...I guess she'd heard us come in...and you backhanded her. Kiaran laid her over there and left right away. He said something about getting Dad and someone named Caroline. And he said he'd send Dad to us."

Almost as if he'd summoned him, his dad was in the room with them. Elam handed him a blanket, which he wrapped around Essie and himself and then leaned back against the chair. He wanted to scream out his frustrations, but his dad was speaking to him.

"I want you to tell me what you know about the room. Everything." He looked at Kiaran and his dad nodded at him. "He was there, he said, but he was more concerned with you. But he couldn't see anything but you. Where was the room, Asher? You have to remember."

"In a cave. There were thirteen people standing around a dais all dressed in black. They were chanting, but I couldn't really hear what they were saying. Essie was there, tied...no, now that I think about it, she was chained to the thing, her body covered in this gold like dust. Even her hair was saturated in it." He closed his eyes and tried to remember every detail. "There was a woman. She called

Essie the child of dragons, and that she was to give it to her. That it was hers."

"Did she say what it was?" Opening his eyes, he shook his head at his dad. "What was she dressed in? Black? Red? What?"

"A black robe that tied in the back. There were lilies down the front of it and all along the hem at the bottom. There was a leather strap that hung down her shoulder to her left hip. It was heavy looking, with a long blade handle at the opening of it. There was a...." Asher had to close his eyes again to think what the design was on the pouch. "It was a dragon. But it wasn't right, not in flight but...but it looked as if it were soaring downward, like he was going to nosedive into the earth."

His dad nodded and asked him what else. He told him about the room with the food. "It was fresh food. I mean, in great contrast to the people around the table. The cutlery was polished and the plates were free of dust and dirt. There were flowers in the center, some of them dead, some not. But it was in varying stages of decay. Like some had been added to the vase over a long period."

"The man at the head of the table. Do you know what he looked like? Did you see a ring? Maybe a part of the crown that might have been something you'd seen before or could recognize again?"

"It was gold; not brightly polished, but I could tell what it was. Rubies were most of the stones in it, except for the one in the center. It was white; not bright, but white with blood lines going through it. There was one on his chest as well, hanging from a long chain that was thick with gold."

"How many people were at the table?" Asher opened his eyes when the woman spoke. He didn't know who she was until she smiled at him. "You helped me once. I want to return the favor. I'm Caroline, the white witch of the Regnum Autem Dracones: or the Kingdom of Dragons. You saved me from the troll several weeks ago."

"How can you help me? Help us? It was a dream, right?" She sat down and shook her head. "But she isn't hurt. Essie is fine. Except that I hurt her when I hit her."

Caroline put out her hand and touched the bruise on Essie's forehead. She woke up and stared at him for several seconds before she cried out and wrapped her arms around him. She was sobbing and Asher held her, fighting his own tears. Caroline stood up, as did the others.

"Dress and come downstairs. I need to hear the story from the beginning. And so you know, this is a foretold dream. Your wife is very strong herself, and has seen enough to help us save all our lives." With that everyone left them.

Asher held Essie for as long as she'd let him before she pulled back and looked at his face.

"You were crying out. I tried to wake you and you were so afraid." He nodded, not able to speak around the tightness in his throat. "I sent Kiaran for someone but when he came back, Jed tried to hold you down, but you were so…you were fighting even him."

"I hit you." She shook her head and put her hand over the bruise that was fading. "Jed said I knocked you off me and you hit your head. I'd never…Kiaran came to me, said it was a dream and that I needed to remember. But when they killed you…oh Essie, I love you so very much."

"I love you too. And I'm just fine." He nodded and pulled her close again. "Asher, we have to see what that woman wants. I have a feeling…I'm not sure what's going on, but I have a feeling that the shit is about to hit the fan."

Laughter wasn't something that he had expected to fall from his mouth, but he felt better for it. Holding Essie just a little longer, he finally let her stand up and watched her dress. She was pulling on a pair of his boxers again when he remembered that Elbert had gone into town for her.

Receiving the clothes filled her with such joy. Watching her put them on and giggling as she showed him how well they fit was the balm that he needed. As soon as she was dressed she went to sit on the bed, because he couldn't let her out of his sight just yet. Everything was too fresh; her death, even though it was a dream, still hurt him.

Chapter 7

"Little is known about the order that you witnessed tonight. Very few people have even seen the ritual that you described and lived to tell about it. And the fact that Essie doesn't remember any of it makes me think that it was your dream and not hers. You were...I'm not sure I completely understand this, but it seems to me that you and her exchanged lives while there."

"I don't understand." Caroline nodded as if she didn't think that they would, and Essie felt stupid. And when she felt that way, she tended to be nasty. "Why is it we're forever playing games with you people? Do you mean that instead of it being me tied to the table, it was Asher and he was seeing me there because...because he couldn't see himself?"

"That's it exactly. You got it. It was his dream, a thing that will come to pass to him and not you. Seeing himself there would have made his mind shut down. But with you being hurt, it was easier for his mind to relax enough to do as Kiaran needed him to do." Essie looked at Asher, who hadn't said a word since he'd told the tale of the room again. He was pale looking, his face drawn. Essie wanted to go to him, hold him, but he looked like he was deep in thought. She hoped that he was trying to forget that he'd hit her, but she was sure he'd never forget that.

"Why him? Not that I want to be tied down naked for a bunch of strangers, but why would this witch, my mother, want something from him?" Caroline looked at Asher, and Essie did too. He was staring at her now and she had a feeling that he'd gotten it worked out.

"They want the dragons. The sign on the bag was something I had seen before. Long ago. It's the death of all dragons. The glyphs on the ceiling, it's there so that the person lying on the dais can read it, a chant. They say it while they're being killed to call the dragons to them. But in my case, I didn't need the words, I have one with me. And she knew it." Caroline told him he was right, but there was more. "Yes. There is lots more. Your mother has been around since the time when dragons roamed the world, like other creatures. She and a group of other fanatics wanted them killed. I don't know why, and if I ever did, I don't remember now. But they formed this…I guess coven, to rid the world of them. The people at the table are the founders. Helena the Black was their witch."

"She was paid nicely to rid the world of dragons too. The money and jewels that she was paid never lasted long, and she had to get more and more creative to find dragons to fall under her spell. Anthony and Eve were strong dragons, and they resisted her every spell for the longest time, it was said. One night, while they reveled in their killing of another fine dragon, Anthony entered their chamber." Caroline raised her hands, and the room they were in seemed to fade out and large dining area appeared. "The king at that time was King Ruben. He was a bad king, raping whoever found themselves close enough for him to fuck, pillaging all the surrounding kingdoms simply to take their women and children. He was not a man, king, or even a human being that was liked."

"When did he reign?" Essie looked at Jacob when he asked. Sometimes Essie forgot that he'd been here when there were kings and queens and a dragon to boot. "The one that I remember wasn't Ruben but someone else. I can't remember him now. Then Anthony."

"His son...Ruben's son, Manchester. He only reigned for a month before Anthony killed him. It was him or the village that he was lord of. Manchester, like his father, was a fool, and a stupid one as well." Caroline smiled at Jacob. "I remember you and Sally. I never came to this home for I knew that it was protected, but I watched you rear your children. It took me a long time to see that you raised the king's hatchlings as well. You did a fine job, the two of you. Sally was a wonderful woman."

"Wait, wait, wait." Everyone turned to Essie when she spoke. "Okay...Jacob, I understand is a ghost. Took me a while to figure that one out, but once I did, things he'd said to me, little things, started to make sense. Elbert was a little harder to get down. He's a shifter, yeah, I get that, but it was the Rottweiler that I never understood until I heard Casdon say it was his preferred animal. I think I saw him as a bird once, and even a big assed bear." Elbert bowed before her and smiled. "But you? You look like you and I are the same age. And you're...you're a white witch. My mother, I get that, is black, but she can't make herself younger, just...I guess, different."

"Your mother is as old as I. Or nearly so. She's younger by a few centuries." Essie shook her head. "Oh, but child, she is. And the reason that you are here now is because I had to work with the queen to make it so. For centuries I had to wait and bide my time until the right man came along to sire you. He had to be this special man, coming into the world at a perfect time. And I had to give Helena the scale to make her conceive you when all the things aligned."

"She knew me." Caroline nodded and turned to Kiaran when she did. Essie stared at the man and the tat on his arm that she knew was there. "When I touched his sigil, it spoke to me. Called me Esmerelda, and told me it was time for me to show them the chamber of gold. I thought…the room is filled with not just gold, but everything. I had thought that was what it meant. But there is a room of gold and she put it there for me to find."

"It was what killed her, taking the gold there for you to find. And with her last breath, she marked Kiaran so that you'd touch him and bring them there."

Essie stood up. It was too much. Everything, her entire life, had been a planned out line of events to bring Asher and Kiaran to a chamber filled with gold. Tears burned her eyes. She'd been manipulated.

"I need some air." She didn't wait for anyone to say anything, but moved to the doorway out onto the yard. Essie didn't want anyone to come with her, and told Asher to give her a few minutes when he stood too. She was hurt and hurting more with each breath she took. When she was outside, Essie took in great gulps of air to try and quell the burning in her heart.

"He doesn't feel that way." She turned to look at Elbert when he spoke. He must have been sitting there when she came out, because he had a cup of tea, a pot with a cozy over it, as well as a plate of scones. "Have some with me, please."

"I need to be alone." He only pushed the filled cup toward her and nodded at the chair. "I was told you were a tea snob. Is that true?"

"It is. I have my own blends that I make. But as for being a snob, I don't drink my brews. I only share them with people that I love. And you, my dear, I love very much. I'll warm your cup while you tell me what you're thinking." She had no idea why she sat down and less why she took the cup when he offered it to her. "Asher loves you."

"Sure he does. Because some queen a long time ago told him that I'd help his family become rich." She knew it was mean and a lie, but she hurt. "People are forever telling me one thing and doing the opposite."

"I had that as well before I worked in the kingdom. His lordship told me he'd be honest with me and he never went back on that promise. His lady wife either." Essie took a sip of the tea and was surprised at the flavor. "This is raspberry. I'm happy to see that you love the taste. I dry the berries myself and then add them to the tea leaves gently so as not to bruise the flavor. Then I add just a touch of lemon to take away the bitterness of the black tea. You do like it, don't you?"

"Yes." She drank her tea in silence for a few minutes until she turned to him. "You said that he doesn't feel that way. What did you mean by that?"

"Kiaran. You thought that he hated you because his mother died putting the gold there for you to show him. I assure you that she only did it because she wanted her sons to have enough to take care of the men who had saved them for her." Essie looked out over the vast fields behind the house and the mountains that seemed to hold it in their palms. "Essie, do you mind if I tell you a story?"

"The woman in there, she told me one as well. Will it be just as farfetched?" He laughed, and she looked at him. "I like you, Elbert. You're a good man, and I think that if you told me something like the other story, I'd believe you."

"Good. And for as much as you'd like to not believe what Lady Caroline is telling you, it's the truth." Essie nodded. She figured it would be. "The story I'd like to tell you is of a young couple. Their names are Anthony and Eve."

"The dragon king and queen." He nodded. "It must have been fantastic living with them, seeing them fly overhead daily. I'm disappointed when I look up and see a plane. I can't imagine what I'd do if I saw a real dragon."

"You see them daily, child. They just don't fly around here so much right now because of the black witch. She is out to kill them, and even before Master Asher's dream, I think they all knew that." Essie nodded and asked him about the couple. "They wanted children. More than anything they wanted to see their children grow into adults and become young men and women. Even as they conceived, they were worried. The witch and the coven were gone now, or so it seemed, and they started their family despite the fear they had about her coming back. A dragon only has a single offspring every thousand years, you see. But Eve had given birth to six of them, a rarity more than anyone would ever have known."

"Did she use magic?" He shook his head. "Then how did she conceive so many and have them? I mean, it seems to me it would weaken her a great deal."

"It did. During most of her pregnancy she had to stay hidden away. If anyone found out or the coven were to rise again, the first thing they'd do was find her and kill her and the unborn hatchlings. So for four months she stayed in the caves. Hiding not just what was happening to her body, but what she was doing as well. Studying the art of witchcraft. With Caroline."

Essie put down her cup and toyed with the cookies on the plate. To eat one, she knew, would be heaven. These were blueberry not the strawberry ones she'd had before, but she knew they'd be just as good.

"When did she figure out that all was not right in her world?" He told her a month before she was due to have the hatchlings. "So she worked through the nights and brought all she could to the chamber and hid it away."

"Yes, they both did. If nothing came to pass, they would have it hidden away for themselves. If there was trouble, it would be for their children. Then on the night after the children were born, she took to the skies with Anthony. They were having so much fun despite what had just happened the day before with the storm, and flying around looking at the damage did little to dispel their happiness. Six sons; they were to have six young dragons to keep them happy in the coming years." He took a sip of his tea as he continued. "The arrow hit her first, piercing her chest through and through. As she fell to the earth, Anthony followed her. His only thought was to save his wife. But the second blade hit him in the chest, not quiet piercing his heart but coming close. As he gathered her into his arms, flying high to be safe, she convinced him to take her to the lair. She wanted to say good-bye to their children. But before he could take her there she was hit again and again, and she was near death when he laid her down."

Tears filled Essie's eyes as she thought about their love. So much of it to be destroyed by one person. And it was her mother. She turned to Elbert as he continued his tale.

"He'd been hit as well; his armor at his chest was exposed now, and he knew that one more hit there and he'd be dead. But Eve told him that he must go to the palace. To lure them away from her and the children. She knew that she was all but dead, as did he, but he left her to do as she'd asked. When he got to the castle, I had already brought Jacob and Sally to him. He'd told me that he needed to see them." Essie wiped at her tears, as did Elbert. "Jacob is a good man, and Sally was very special as well. She was a powerful witch in her own right, and her sister is as well."

"Caroline." Elbert smiled and nodded. "This is like a never ending circle of people touching each other's lives."

"It is a world of safety for all that are in the circle, Essie. Each person touched by this tale, this story is a part of them. Each of them have their parts to play, and if they are not played out, then things never can get to the end. Lady Eve knew this, as did her husband the king. Touching the lives before they were born, manipulating things so that her family would be safe, all of this and more is the way of the world, the way to your heart." He touched the ring on her finger. "This was Lady Eve's, did you know that? She wore it every day. I never saw her without it once in all the time I worked there. To see it on your hand now, a gift not just from the man who loves you, but the children of the woman who needed you, makes me know that things are going to work out for the best, and with you here, nothing can go wrong."

"I'm not as positive as you are." He laughed and she looked at him. "You're a very nice man. Do they appreciate you enough?"

"They do. And I have the friendship of one that I admire very much." She asked him who that would be. "You, my dear. I have you as a friend, and I do admire you.

When I think of all that you have gone through in the past weeks, my heart soars with love for you. You are a good fit in this house."

"I don't fit well with anyone, Mr. Elbert. I have been...you know who my mother is. You know what she is." Essie laughed, and even to her own ears it sounded bitter and harsh. "You can't even say that I was born of love. Not even a mistake. I was planned by a woman so far removed from my life that I don't even have a clue what she looked like."

"I love you." Essie turned to look at Asher. He was standing in the doorway looking like a man who simply belonged here in this lovely old rich house. He didn't look at Elbert when he spoke again. "Elbert, can you see what you can do about dinner? Caroline has decided to stay for a while, and everyone is wanting to have steaks on the grill."

"I can do that." Elbert stood and kissed her on the cheek. "I love you as well, my dear. Very much so. And I'm glad to have you as part of this family."

He left them there, and Essie wasn't sure what to say. Remaining on the chair where she'd been, she watched as Asher took the other. He took one of the scones and broke it in half, and she took part of it while he ate the other part. When he finished he reached over, picked her up, and put her on his lap.

"I'm so very sorry." She asked him for what and hated that she was getting teary again. "For everything. Hitting you for the most part, bringing you into this. But I guess that wouldn't have been me, but my dad. He's just told us that he didn't know who you were, but he liked you when you cursed at him for sneaking up on you."

"I was in the barn. There were newborn kittens in there and I was looking at them, when suddenly this man says to me in a sharp voice not to touch them. He scared ten years off my life." Asher laughed, as did she at the memory. "The mother, he told me, was very territorial, and she'd not accept them if I touched them. I told him that I'd touched them while she was there, and she didn't seem to mind. He sat with me and talked about you and your brothers the rest of the afternoon. Then he invited me into the house for some lunch."

"I was brought here under the guise of resting up. I'd been a little stressed lately." He kissed her mouth quickly as he continued. "Best rest I get is when I come deep inside of you, while you scream out my name."

He kissed her again, this time slower, his mouth making the rest of her body hum with need. She wanted him to take her, right now, but she knew that there were others around...most of them just inside the house in the kitchen.

"Asher, what are we going to do about this? If what Caroline says is true, and I'm thinking she's right, my mother is going to come for you guys and hurt the dragons." He nodded but said nothing. "You were so afraid when you were asleep. All I could think of was that someone was trying to kill you."

"She was. She wanted me to tell her where they were, I think. And the more I think about it, the more I've come to realize she has no idea that we're one and the same." Essie sat up, something just occurring to her. "What is it?"

She went into the house and saw Caroline. There was something she'd said to her that made her think she knew more than she was saying. As soon as she looked at her, Essie knew she did.

"Who is he?" Caroline smiled and bowed. "My father. You said that he was special, that he had his own magic. Who is he and where is he?"

She turned to Elbert. Essie fell back but said nothing. Caroline didn't move either, but Elbert took a step toward her. When she took another step back, he stopped but spoke to her.

"He knew what was going on when I asked him to lay with her. I knew…it was to bring you into the world." He glanced at Caroline before he looked at her again. "I didn't know who you were when I got here. In fact, I didn't have any idea that you were even around this area. I had wanted to watch over you for him. Care for you, but it would not have been helpful to you. She, Helena, would have harmed you; or more than likely killed you. I didn't figure it out until you said she was your mother. I have let him know since you've come here."

"Who is he? Where did he…what was he? Do you have any idea what you all left me with her? Knowing what kind of evil-assed person she was, and no one came to help me?" Essie wiped at the useless tears as she stood there. "Do you have any idea what she did to me? How she…for days on end she would try her magic on me. Make me lure people to the house so that she could experiment on them too. Then one day when I was twelve, I decided that I'd had enough, fuck that shit and her, and left. I've had to…I've been alone for sixteen years."

"You're not now." Elbert came to her again and she had nowhere to go. "Come, child. We're here for you now. All of us. And I know that it sounds trite, but being with her has made you what you are today. A very strong woman who can hold your own."

"I'm not...I don't...." She was sobbing now. Her heart felt as if they'd torn if from her chest and stomped it. Then for good measure, they'd burned the sucker too. "I want to leave here. I want to...I don't know where I'm going, but I need to leave."

Asher came up behind her and put his hands on her shoulders. He held her no matter how hard she tried to shake him off. Then he kissed her shoulder. His breath on her neck made her shiver and distracted her from her pain.

"I want you to think. Okay?" She nodded. "Okay. Close your eyes and just breathe for me. In and out, and listen to me."

"Asher, I—" He hushed her and told her to listen to his voice. To think about only that. She did, but she was so upset that she was sure that whatever he was doing wasn't going to work.

"We're going to take control now. You and I are going to have a life together. You have brothers now. Some you're not going to like so much, but you have them. There's Elbert and my father here for you. Dragons as well. We're all here for you." She started to turn and see if he was serious, but he held her. "You can't die, Essie. Your mother can. She's only an immortal because she uses magic. You're immortal because of the magic that's in your blood. Once we figure out what you are, we're going to work on you learning the magic that you inherited too."

"I don't want to have magic." But she did, and she was pretty sure he knew it. "Can I shift? Into a dragon? I mean, can I take on the shape of a dragon?"

"I don't know." They both looked at Elbert, and he shook his head.

"So, I can't shift into a dragon. Or anything else, right?"

"You can be anyone you want or need to be. Anyone." Elbert nodded to Asher as he continued. "You can do what he cannot because of your magic, but becoming a dragon will not be one of them. You can take on shapes of others but you cannot become one. You are...you are everything."

He said that like she should know what he meant, but she had no idea. Then Akassa, Simeon's dragon, laughed, and she looked at him. He pointed to Caroline, who was grinning as if she knew as well.

"I don't get it." No one said anything, and she looked at Jacob when he entered the room with them. "They are being very vague and I'm starting to get pissed."

As Akassa told him what was going on, Jacob turned to her. He was grinning too. "Why, my dear, you could be the dragon bitch that takes out the black witch once and for all."

She looked at Asher. "You think I can kill her? I mean, just kill her before she harms you?"

"I do. You're very strong now. And as Kiaran told me the other day, you have a great deal of your own magic that you use all the time." She shook her head. "Yes, you do. Put out your hand and think of the tea that Elbert just made."

Her fingers were trembling, but she did what he said with Elbert instructing her on what to do. When the cup touched her fingers, she realized she'd closed her eyes and missed it. She started to ask if someone had done it, but she thought of the cup going back to Elbert and it did. She giggled.

"Holy shit, I have magic."

Chapter 8

Helena was leaning over her pots when she realized that she was hungry. Starved actually. She'd been trying for days now to come up with a poison that would not just kill the woman off, but bring that other creature with her when she died. But it was the other man, the one that walked the fields in shadows, that made her afraid.

She'd seen him three times in the last few days, always out in the fields beyond her home, and even into the other property that she couldn't go and get him. Someone had put a protective shield around the place, and she could no longer get close to the house or anyone there. She wasn't sure who he was or why he was there, but she knew that somehow he was with the woman there. If only her daughter, the spawn of her loins, were there to go into the house and find out what was going on.

She'd never wanted the thing. Her daughter had been conceived because Helena had been stupid enough to think she was too old. Well, not too old, but certainly much too old to conceive a child. And with that man.

It had been her plan when she'd come with him the first time to kill him when she was finished, but she never got the chance. Helena knew that he was powerfully magical, of course. You couldn't let a man fuck you all night long and into the next afternoon without at least knowing that much. But where he'd been from or who he might have worked for had never been a concern...until she'd seen him again recently.

He had been walking through her yard on that fateful day when she'd had the urge to take him. And she had too. Christ, it was as if she couldn't get him naked fast enough, or inside of her soon enough either. She'd thrown him to the ground and was coming almost as soon as his cock was free.

And what a cock he'd had, too. Stiff and thick. She'd come three times before he'd tossed her to her back and plowed her hard. When he came inside of her, crying out his own release, she thought him done, but she wasn't nearly finished with him. As soon as he pulled his still hard cock from her, she'd taken him into her mouth to keep him hard until he was ready again.

They'd never made it to the bedroom of her shack, but had had sex all over the rest of the house and in the yard, porch, as well as on the fence that once surrounded her home. Sometimes twice. When he'd left her the next day, she'd been pleased to see him limping slightly, and got up to bath him off her. It was then that she'd realized that he'd planted a child in her, and that there was no way for her to rid herself of it. And his magic was beyond her reach now.

But she'd tried. Over the next several months she'd done everything she could think of to expel the issue. Nothing worked. It was as if the thing had attached itself to her and wasn't leaving until it was finished growing.

When it was an infant, she'd had to feed it or listen to it cry all the time. It hadn't been picky about the milk it had, taking the cows' milk when she had one, or even a goat when it came too close to the house. Then when it had gotten older, the thing had made its way into the yard and got her own food. After that…well, she supposed, she'd lost track of it, because one day she noticed that the girl was gone. Not even a note to thank her for birthing her into this world.

She'd called her Esmerelda because it had sounded like an evil name. Not that there were any birth certificates with the child, but it did need a name. Especially when she used the chit to bring her people she could experiment on.

Esmerelda had hated it too. Helena supposed that was why she'd used her…the way that she'd look at her when she'd told her what she wanted her to do. Then she'd make her sit and watch her dissecting the people, taking out the choicest parts to use, and even had her discard the rest of the bodies. Helena had learned a great deal about the human body then, and had actually missed Esmerelda when she'd disappeared like she had. And now that she had a use for her again, Helena had no idea where to find her.

Sitting out on her porch, she looked over at the property beyond hers. Helena had since realized that whatever she'd seen in the sky had been a flock of birds. There were no more dragons in this world, she and her friends had seen to that.

King Ruben had been…he'd been a good lay, and sometimes when she had looked down at Esmerelda, she wished she'd been his. The man had been pure evil and could be a sadist at times, which would make even her a little on the nervous side. But he'd funded her and had the chamber built for them to worship.

Helena had never forgotten that either. Each time they went to the chamber, other beings like her, she'd make sure there were plenty of things for the king and his court. Every month at the new moon they'd gather together, not just to sacrifice new blood to him and the goddess that they worshiped, but to pay homage to him as well. It was a shame that that bastard had killed them all.

Helena had never participated in the meals with them. It was too rich for her tastes and some of the food was…well, unclean as far as she was concerned. No, when they ate she would clean the altar and make things ready for the next time they were together. The night that they had been killed she'd been on the altar with her legs spread wide with the king's son, Manchester. He'd been flirting with her all night long, and she needed to have a nice fuck before going home.

He'd not been all that good with sex. He'd been more concerned with his own release than that of the person he was with. And it mattered little to him if it was male or female. Or, for that matter, if there were more than one of them. He would fuck until he was finished, then simply pull away and leave her there. But that night he'd been particularly horny and she'd had her own release before he'd finished. When he'd finished, he'd stood over her with his head cocked.

"What is it?" He asked her if she could hear anything. "No. Should I? I mean, did you expect angels to sing for you when you emptied your balls?"

He laughed, then told her he did. "But listen. Do you hear my father? I mean, he's noisy enough to wake the dead when he's in his cups. What do you hear?"

Helena would forever think that he killed them all. He'd been plowing her, and after she'd given it some thought, he'd been loud as well. She knew that he was covering the noises of them dying in the other room. Pulling on her clothes, she followed him to the dining chamber and could see that all of them were dead, or very close to it.

"Did you do this?" She shook her head at his question. "They've been poisoned. Look at the mess they've made when they ate the beef."

He'd known too much. Not only did he know that the beef had been poisoned and it was her that brought it to the chamber, he also knew that the wine had been tainted as well. She knew it then, and had never forgotten the look of glee on his face when he told her that she'd just fucked the king. But when they entered the kitchen that had cooked the food, there had been enough dead bodies in there as well that she figured that whoever was in with him would have no problems killing a witch too. Even one as strong as she was.

Helena went out onto her porch to think things over. She had several pots simmering near the fire, and it was simply too hot for her to think about too much today. As soon as she sat down, the thoughts of Manchester came back to her.

He'd been worse than his father, and who would have thought that even possible? Not her, and more than likely not the peoples of the village. But he had been, and in the few months, less than three if she remembered correctly, he'd done more damage to the castle, killed more people than his father, and had ran through most of the kingdom's monies. Not that it didn't thrill her to no end to have Anthony come into the kingdom broke as a mouse, but he did seem to be able to turn things around quickly.

Anthony and his wife had been…she supposed good leaders. They had been known to go into the homes of the sick to comfort them. And twice she knew that he'd gone to the fields of some farmer to help him bring his crops in when there just wasn't enough help. But there was something about them that she did not trust. And it turned out, she was right.

They were dragons, the very thing that she hated more than she did anything else. And the fact that they were magical in their own right pissed her off even more. She wanted them dead. She wanted their bodies too.

The dragon was useful in so many ways. Not only were the scales strong enough to shield a body from harm, but when ground into potions and other medicinal spells, it would enhance beauty, cure eye sight, and even at times, if used properly, be used to change the appearance. For a price of course. She'd be rich beyond her dreams.

The horns could be cut up and used as elixirs, for too many things for her mind to think of. Their blood had abilities that would bring someone back from near death, as well as give long life to someone who drank it daily. The others that she'd killed, four in all her lifetime, had been used up, their properties long gone when she'd found out what the king and queen were. And she'd have them both.

The storm had nearly exhausted her the day she'd conjured it. It was all she'd been able to do to get to the hillside to see the people two days later, and tell them that the king and queen had done it all with their magic. Getting them to storm the castle hadn't been her idea at first. She'd only wanted them to wait until they were out again to kill the king and queen, but someone had suggested it and she'd fueled the flames, so to speak.

The men in the group were set to split into two groups. They knew where the queen was, they'd said. And as they went off to kill her, the king and queen flew overhead and had them all going after them. She wished she'd been there to see her fall. The great dragon queen would have made such a spectacular site falling to the ground dead.

But she never made it to either of their downfalls. She'd been knocked to the ground by someone and her head had been split open. Already weakened from the use of all her magic, it had taken her days after the castle came down, and more weeks after that, before she could even touch the wound without spilling her belly on the ground. Still, all these centuries later, she could still feel the jagged scar that had been the death of all her dreams.

Helena was just about to go in and see to her pots when she saw a shadow again. This time she made sure that she was out where she could see it, and nearly fell back to the ground when she looked up. It was a dragon...she'd bet her life on it, and the thing was beautiful.

She had no idea where he might have come from...the mountains, she supposed. But he was headed towards the ruins, and she decided to follow it. Hurrying to make sure nothing on the fire would burn or bubble over, she grabbed up her things and her potions and took off. By the time she got there, breathing heavily and having a stitch in her side, she couldn't find him.

"Damn, damn, damn." Getting as close to the ruins as she could, she walked around them. The spell here—or ward, she supposed—that held the place safe prevented her from actually going onto the grounds, but she could move around the outer edge and see enough to know that he wasn't there. Just as she decided that she was going back to her home, he appeared with a man.

They were too far away for her to hear, but she could see that they were good friends. Her mind was working on how to get them into her lair when she saw something that had her going deeper within the woods. There weren't just one of them, there were six.

Six dragons, all of them of different hues of golds and browns. The men with them meant nothing to her, because if she could only get half the dragons, she'd be set up for a very long time. And she'd be the envy of every witch still alive. Helena had to make herself stand still by holding onto the tree she stood next to. It would do her no good to show herself now.

For over an hour she watched them. The dragons moving large stones with their huge claws, and the men searching through the rubble. It wasn't until she was ready to leave that she saw the woman again. Helena watched how they all seemed to cater to her every whim, and one of the dragons even fanned her with his great wings, much to the amusement of the others.

Taking note of every detail of her, Helena's mind was working out a plan to get the dragons to come to her. She'd have to wake the coven again, long since dormant because of the lack of dragons. Then she'd have to clean the chambers, or at least have them cleaned. What were servants for if not to do the manual labor, she thought?

As she left the area, fearful that she'd be seen before her work had begun, she thought of all the ways she could lure the girl to her. It would be easy too. Girls like that one would be too nice to let something like helping someone pass her by.

A little old woman needing help with something or other. She might even give herself a limp, or even a cane. Picking up a long willow stick, she turned it into a cane as she moved through the woods to her home. The dress she had on began to fade, from what she had on to a worn patched dress with an old stained apron. Her hair, her lovely hair that she thought her crowning glory, was left to go to its original color. The white gray flowed down her back to nearly her hips as she thought of her voice.

Helena had a cracked voice to begin with. Even as a child it had sounded like she'd eaten a chicken whole and he'd taken over her sound box. Her breasts grew as she stepped onto her property until they sank a little under her shift. Helena even put a little scar at her throat to show that she'd been through a great deal in all her years. She was cackling when she entered her house, gleeful of what she was going to gain in riches very soon.

~~~

Abraham was sitting on the porch of their home when they returned. He'd not seen such a sight as dragons flying since he'd been a younger man. It was a sight that he knew very few would ever see in their lifetime if he had not seen the witch in his daily walks.

As they approached him and the house, he stood up. The only person that he actually knew was Elbert, and he wasn't among the group. Cautious that he made no quick or sudden moves, Abraham tried to look as calm as he could when the first dragon spit a line of fire at him.

"You know me to be without malice, or I would not be so close to the house." The dragon didn't spit again, but they circled around the men with them and looked like something from his worst nightmares. "I come to see Elbert. He is my friend and I have news of the witch."

The man that came from the circle looked so much like his father that it nearly took his breath away. This man was the son of Jacob and Sally, he'd bet his life on it. And if this was true, then Abraham's own child might be with them.

"Elbert has gone to the mountains to gather herbs. If you are a friend of his, I'd like to know his relationship to you." If he was correct about the man before him, he also knew his name. "And who are you?"

"You're Asher Anthony. A man named for the ruins of the castle from which you were given life, and a great king like none other." The man nodded but didn't speak. "You have five brothers, all of them holders of the dragons of said king and his lovely wife. Men of a breed like none other. I am Abraham, father to the daughter given to you from the queen."

She was there then, stepping from behind the dragons and standing next to Asher. He nearly stepped to her, but she walked slowly to him, Asher matching her steps with his own. When she stood in front of the porch, Abraham moved down the two steps to get a better look at her. She was beyond lovely. She was the most beautiful —

The fist that hit him in the nose knocked him back on the steps. Before he could figure out what he'd done, she was telling him to stand up so that she could hit him again. He looked up at her from his prone position and realized that she was furious. And a fighter.

"I said to get up. I'm not nearly done with you." Abraham looked at Asher, but he would be no help with the woman. He was laughing so hard that he was holding his belly. "Are you going to get up or am I going to have to kick you while you're down?"

"What are you upset with me about? And for the record, my dear, I shall lay here until you are over your snit." She kicked him in the ribs, and he had to hold them for fear that she'd break a few of them with her booted foot. "Stop this."

"You fucking left me there." He had to move back from her fury or be injured again when she tried to kick him again. "You just fucked her, knowing that I'd be born, then you never returned. Get up."

"Esmerelda." Abraham looked at the man who spoke. Elbert looked like a man who was trying his best not to burst something, and his humor was spilling out over his face. "He's your father. Have some respect."

The foot connected with his head. Abraham tried his best to hold onto his consciousness, but the darkness won out. His last thoughts were that he'd have to make this up to her, and that she was a hell of a warrior.

When he woke next, he was laying on a bed. He looked around the room before rising, and saw his Esmerelda sitting in the chair next to his bed. Abraham took this time, when she was unaware of him, to look at her.

Her hair was as dark as the night. Straight like his, but with a little curl at the end of her gathered hair. Her eyes, if he remembered correctly, were the blue of the sky. Still, he was fairly certain that with all her beauty, he would never want her to draw against him in a fight.

"You done?" Her voice cut through his thoughts, and he sat up to look at her. "I was told that I had to tell you that I'm sorry. I'm not, but they didn't say I had to be sincere about it. So, I'm sorry that I didn't hit you harder."

Abraham couldn't help it. He laughed. Christ, she was as ill-tempered as his mother on her good days, and just as cutting as his father when he was without his morning brew. She glared harder at him, then stood. Abraham actually stiffened in anticipation of her hitting him again.

"Do they call you Esmerelda or something less formal?" She told him her name. "It suits. You're very pretty, I'm sure you know that."

"What I know or don't know is none of your business." True, but he didn't comment as she continued. "She was a horrible mother to me. If what she was could be considered a mother. You should have come back for me."

"I wasn't able to. Once I fathered you as the queen requested, I was put into a deep sleep by Caroline to heal. A hibernation, as it were. Lying with the witch harmed me in ways that you cannot imagine." She asked him how. "My body was burned and my insides were...she is as acidy inside as she is out."

He could see her blush and hated to have done it to her, but he wanted her to understand that he would not have abandoned her if he could have prevented it. Sitting up, he swung his legs over the side of the bed and stretched. There was much to tell them all, but for now, he thought being with his daughter was much more important.

"You're not human." He shook his head and nearly pointed out that neither was she when she continued. "Asher said that I have magic inside of me. I've been playing with it, but I can't seem to get anything to work right. I don't suppose you'll hang around long enough to show me a thing or two to beat the witch."

"I want to hang around, but you should know that you're not a witch." Essie just stared at him. "Neither am I. Helena is one; not because she was born one, but she just knows some spells. And she's killed a great many other witches that were very good at what they did to gain their powers. Without that, she'd be just as normal as most humans."

"And the dragons? Why does she want them dead?" He was surprised by the fact that she knew, and he could see that she was pleased by that. "She's going to take Asher and kill him if I can't figure out a way to kill her first. Because she is not getting to my family. Not like she did me."

"She won't." Abraham stood up, and she didn't back away from him this time. "I'm going to help you with your magic. I think...no, I know that you can beat her at her own games. But if she gets even one of your dragons, Essie, all will be lost."

"Nothing will be lost, Abraham, or I will die trying." He nodded. Abraham was proud of her in that moment, but thought it best if he said nothing. Their relationship was not one of good faith as yet. But he knew he would win her over. Or, as she said, he would die trying. He followed her out of the room to the kitchen.

Chapter 9

Asher watched the two of them in the yard. When Kiaran and Onimia came and sat beside him, he didn't speak but continued to look at Abraham and Essie move about. It was frustrating watching her fall back when some of Abraham's magic touched her, but he told her he'd behave.

"Have you been sent here so she can work without you trying to protect her? Or you here for the entertainment value?" He looked at Onimia and told him entertainment. "She is doing well, but he is not a good teacher. He's afraid of hurting her."

"He has a few times." Onimia nodded. "You think you can help her? Because she is getting really pissed at how slowly this is going. I don't think she wants to be excellent at it all now, but he's been on the same two things for over an hour, and I'm afraid she's going to bash his head in again."

Onimia got up and walked toward the student and teacher. Asher sat up. He had no idea what was going to happen, but he was sure it was going to be good. Kiaran laughed and Asher looked at him.

"I think that before this is done, Onimia is going to be glad he's an immortal." Asher laughed too. "I don't think Abraham is going to give him the field. What do you think...? She's going to kick his ass again, or do you suppose she's going to give into her dad?"

"I think she's going to take Onimia to the ground." Bets were placed on not *if* she would but *when* she would. Kiaran said she'd fall first, then Onimia, but Asher thought she'd take them both down, Onimia and Abraham, before either of them left the field.

"You should know that you can hurt me, but not kill me." Essie nodded at Onimia. Abraham was telling them both that he had it, but Essie looked at Onimia when he took a stance and told her to do the same. "You have power in your body. And you can pull from the earth. I want you to kick off your shoes and try to—"

"She's not ready for that. Her strength is too strong right now, and if you add the elements to it, she's going to hurt herself." Abraham stepped between Onimia and Essie, and Asher laughed. The men were going to be hurt more than she would. "Look, Essie. Just try and use the power like I've been showing you."

Essie kicked off her shoes, and Asher reached into the earth himself and asked it to help her. Their reply was that she was helping them, so they'd be honored to help her out. Asher could see the power running up her body. The grass at her feet seemed to grow an inch as soon as she dug her feet deep. Asher knew whatever was going to happen now wasn't going to be because he'd asked the earth anything, but her own willpower and magic.

Asher could see the exact moment that she could feel it. Her face was bright with the power, and her body was humming. He started to tell her to back it down, to ease it from her hands, but she was lifting them to the two men and blasting them across the yard before he could. Well, Asher supposed, he could have warned them, but this was too much fun. Getting up, he went to her.

Putting his arms around her waist, he leaned into her ear. "Heal them. Just reach deep into the earth and ask for its help. Always ask, because there might be something going on that they cannot help you." She nodded. "Now, bring Onimia to you."

He was surprised at the ease with which she did it. As she lifted him up, his body hurt but not broken, she brought him to her and laid him gently on the ground. He sat up and winked at her. When she brought Abraham to her, laying him down as well, he could see that the man was hurt worse, but not enough to be unable to stand. When he did, he glared at Onimia.

"I told you she couldn't handle it. She's going to hurt herself and others until she can get the hang of this. Being an elemental faerie takes years of practice." No one moved. Asher looked at Kiaran when he stepped in front of Essie when he did. "I told you she wasn't human."

"You never said what she was." An elemental faerie? Christ, Asher was stunned at the amount of magic that she held. "You said faerie. Nothing more. Do you have any idea what Helena would do with her if she knew?"

"It's why no one knows what either of us are." Abraham looked saddened by what he'd just confessed. "No one knew. Not even Elbert when he asked me to father her. The queen did, I suppose, but no one...we're the last of them. Even as a half-breed, as she is, she's more powerful than any witch. And a witch will want her magic."

Asher felt her touch his arm. When she stepped between him and Kiaran, he could see that something was different. And when she turned and looked at him, he took a step back. She had it. He had no idea what it was or who had given it to her, but Essie had it all.

This time when she lifted her hand, she pointed it to the smallish tree in the yard...a sapling that had been there from the mighty oak nearby. Her fingers danced at the end of her hand, and he watched with the rest of them as the tree grew, its branches growing and strengthening until it was as big as the one next to it.

Buds formed at the end of each branch and along the bark. Then leaves, dark green and full, unrolled from each one and opened to the sun. Acorns filled the tree then, tiny seeds that would take root, he knew, and grow magnificent trees like its sire. When it was finished, the tree at full grown, she turned to him and smiled.

"The earth said it would help me." He nodded without speaking, not even sure if he could at this point. "She said that you guys were taking too long and there was business afoot. I really like her. She also said that if I needed anything else, I was to just ask. It was her pleasure to help me."

"I bet it was." Asher looked at Abraham as he felt his anger take a step up. "You should have told us. We have to take better care of her now. And not just because she's new at this, but you know what Helena will do to her if she gets her now."

"She'll take her powers. And that of the dragons." Asher asked Abraham how. "Because even if you don't realize it just yet, Asher, you are the king of all dragons, even the ones that are not here. And if Helena gets Essie, you will give her whatever she wants to save your bride."

"Not here? I don't understand." Asher looked at Kiaran and Onimia. "Do you know what he's talking about?

Caroline said she was the leader of the dragons. I can't be the king of anything."

"No, what she said was, she was the witch of the dragons' kingdom. That doesn't make her the leader; you are. And yes, I think I understand what Abraham is saying," Onimia said with a grin. "I think he's telling you that you're the big boss of us all, and that there are more than just the six of us. And so you know, I've always known that you were going to be the leader, along with Kiaran. It's just he thinks you can do this on your own. But we all know that the two of you are going to bring us back."

Asher was almost afraid to ask him bring them back from what, but he didn't have to. Kiaran answered him for Onimia. "There are more of us than the six here now. Not many. In fact, there are less than a dozen of us all told. I knew that a few days ago, just after we arrived here. They're...I guess you could call it calling to me. And the others. They won't come until the witch is taken care of, but they'll come. This is the safest place for them until we can find them hosts."

"You mean they all need hosts?" Kiaran nodded, and Asher looked at Onimia, who nodded as well. "How the hell am I supposed to find them hosts? Mine was preordained for me. Are you saying that these other dragons have someone out there that's just for them as well?"

"No." Abraham laughed when Asher huffed at him. "You and your wife, you are surely suited. No, they are not preordained. It wasn't until you and the others came back here that things started to be put into motion. I wouldn't be surprised if some, if not all of them, are on their way right now."

Asher looked around. He noticed then that Essie was missing. When he started for the house, he saw her. She was sitting in the glen just behind the house, looking up at the sky as she sat in the grass. Kiaran leaned to him and spoke, his voice just a whisper as he told him what she was doing.

"She's learning. If I were you, I'd let her go. She cannot be harmed on the property, and she will need this information in the coming days." Asher asked him why that soon as he continued to watch her. "The witch has seen us. She knows that we're here. Abraham spied her looking at us at the ruins. It's why he's here."

"You mean that he's seen her?" Kiaran nodded. "Then she has more than likely seen him. So she'll figure out that Essie is his daughter and hers."

"And?" Asher let his mind wander over the implications of what this might mean. "She knows that Essie is her daughter anyway. What does that change?"

"Essie doesn't look like the child that left her. She's…she's so much different that if I were to see her as a child, I'd not know her as the adult. The witch has no clue that the woman that she has seen is the child she gave birth to." Asher looked at Kiaran, wondering how the hell that was possible. "Look at her, Asher; even now she looks different with the power of her magic. Helena is going to know that, and when she finally realizes what she's up against, it will be too late for her to back off."

"You mean that Essie will kill her." Kiaran didn't answer but looked at the field beyond. "She'll try, won't she? No matter if I ask her not to, she'll have to try and save us all."

"I believe that it, like our entire life, is written out and we are going to have to wait for it to play out to see how it ends." Then Kiaran shifted, his dragon taking shape almost in a heartbeat. *I believe that without her, all will be lost anyway.*

Asher had a feeling that he was right. He didn't like it but knew it was right. All would be lost without her help. And he'd be lost without her by his side.

~~~

Essie lay in the grass and stared up at the sky. When a shadow fell across her, she moved her head so that she could see who was standing over her. She really wasn't surprised to see Mr. Jacob. He sat beside her and he touched his finger over the flower that she'd broken. When he showed it to her, she could see that it was now repaired and it seemed to have grown a little.

"It was a gift to me from his mother. I think us both having the ability to use the earth was passed onto Asher in a way that was stronger than both of us." She nodded but didn't say anything as Mr. Jacob spoke again. "You're even stronger than he is. And that's a good thing. You'll be able to control things that…well, I can't imagine what you'll be able to control with this."

"I'm a faerie." Jacob nodded. "I'm not sure what the hell that means to me. I mean…I guess it's a good thing and the earth said that I'd be helping them a lot. I don't suppose you know what she means."

"I do know that my wife, rest her soul, used to tell me that when you borrow from the earth that you had to pay it back times ten. She would cut some herbs and put her hand in the soil and thank it. I'm not real sure what she was doing when she did that, but she was happy and that is all that mattered to me. But I do know that when she picked mushrooms, which was her favorite pastime, she'd take a little of our leftovers with her to put on the mound as a little extra for them." Essie nodded. She could see that. But the rest? Not so much. "You'll get it, dear. You'll have lots of time to practice."

They sat there for a little while, and she thought of all the things that had happened to her recently. "Mr. Jacob, did you use magic to make me fall in love with Asher?"

"No." He sat there playing in the grass. "I don't know if I could have or not, but no, I didn't use it. What I did do was bring two people together that mean a great deal to me."

"I like you. A great deal too." He nodded and grinned at her. When she sat up suddenly, he started to speak but she put her hand up. "There's something...like a disturbance going on. In the valley near...I think the ruins."

Closing her eyes, she stood up. Her shoes were still off, so she dug her toes into the dirt and listened. It was strange at first. She was actually listening to the dirt. She knew that the others had come to her. She didn't know if Jacob had called them or something else, but they were standing close when she opened her eyes.

"It's not the ruins, but close by. There's a mountain about two miles from the ruins that has a deep cavern in it. The earth said that there is black magic going on, but she can hide from it. She said that the mountain told her that it has not happened in many winters." Asher took her hand, and she could feel a power surge run up her arm. "Christ, do you feel that?"

"Listen," Asher told her. Closing her eyes again, she listened and was happy to feel the mountain speaking. Asher held her hand and then her body to his, cradling it as he whispered in her ear. "If you ask him, he'll let you see what you need to see. But be gentle. It's his first time too."

Nodding, she asked the mountain to show her the disturbance. And as it faded into her vision, she could see the large room.

"I think it's the room that Asher was in. There's a dais in the middle of the room and markings on the wall that I don't...I can't read them." Asher told her he could, but to look around. She moved all around the room, telling them about the things she could see. Then she came to a locked door and went through it. "It's a tomb. There are thirteen bodies in different stages of decay. They're not...there is no seal at the end of their resting place."

As she stood there, looking over the bodies and trying to figure out what the hell she was seeing, the door behind her opened and there stood her mother. Asher tightened his grip on her waist, but he never spoke. Neither of them did as her mother moved into the room.

The first body in the topmost tomb moved as she said some words over it. She poured a potion on his head and then uttered more words. Essie told this to the people with her, taking comfort in the fact that she really wasn't in the room with her. As her mother did this to the next body, the first one began to pull himself free of his resting place.

"She's waking them up." Essie had no idea why she knew this to be true, but she watched as her mother woke each of the bodies up until all of them were awake but one. "The tenth one isn't moving. I mean...it looks like his place has been caved in or something. Helena is very pissed."

"What do you mean? Is he dead?" It was a strange question, she supposed, since they were in a tomb to begin with, but it somehow fit. She told Simeon that she thought that was what had happened.

"She's saying how she's going to have to find a new coven member. The first man she woke is nodding, but I can't see his face. I'm thinking I might not want to. But he's mumbling something back to her and she...wait. It's another language. He's speaking to her in something other than English." Essie listened to the man, hoping something would come to her, but there wasn't anything. "I don't know, but Helena told him to go to the next town and find a fresh one. I don't...I think she means a fresh body."

The mountain seemed to need a rest, and she pulled from his place. Thanking him for his help, she told him that the next time she was there, she'd bring him something special. He told her that if she were to remove the blemish within his belly, he'd be happy with that.

"What do we do now?" No one said anything, but they did look strangely at her. When she turned to Asher, he smiled. "What's going on?"

"They're in awe of you." She looked at the other men standing there, and then back at Asher. "They are, love. You just not only spoke to a mountain about five miles from here, but peeked inside of his body and looked around with me hanging on."

Flushing, feeling her face heat up to almost too hot, she looked at Jacob. He was grinning like an idiot. She started to ask him what was so funny when he touched his hand to her arm. The connection was profound, and she was shoved back from it. Rolling over once and landing on her ass, Asher came to help her and she looked at his dad.

Jacob stood there for several seconds, then put out his hand to help her up. She didn't know if she wanted to be hit with that again, but took his hand. She felt him, not just the power but the man himself. When she was standing, Jacob went to Asher and put his hand on his shoulder. Then he pulled him into his arms and hugged his son.

"Oh Dad. How I have missed doing this with you." Asher sobbed as he held his dad to him. The hug turned into another, then another as they pulled back a little only to grab each other again. When Asher let him go finally, Jacob turned to the man standing next to him. Jed didn't look like he was thrilled about this.

"I'm going to be sorely pissed if I can't hug you as well." Jacob nodded, then put his hand on his son's chest. Then before she could say it was working, Jed pulled his dad to him and lifted him off the ground in a big bear hug. They were all sobbing when he sat him back to the ground. "I don't know what happened, but I have to tell you, I've never been happier in my entire life to have had you here."

Each of them got their turn hugging and holding their dad. Even the dragons, all of them men, hugged the man like he was long lost to them. Essie supposed that he was in a sense. But to have that much love for your parent was foreign to her. When Jacob turned to her, she knew that he was going to hug her as well, but he didn't. He looked like…she started crying when he did.

"I cannot tell you what you've done for me." She shook her head. "Yes, you did. I don't know how you did it, but you let me feel again."

"I didn't do anything. You just touched me and it happened." He nodded, tears still streaming down his face. "Mr. Jacob, I'm going—"

"I'd be proud as a speckled pup under a little red wagon if you called me anything other than Mr. Jacob." He touched her cheek and took away one of her tears. "I'd be happy to have you call me 'Dad' if you want. I know you got yourself one, but I'd very much like that too."

Nodding, she was beyond words to express how she felt about the honor of calling him "Dad." She'd never used the term before, not even for her own father. Yes, she did have Abraham, but he was too...she supposed distant would be the best way to describe their relationship. He was there, but more like a man who she knew than anything else.

Jacob hugged her then. Pulled her tightly to his big body and held her to him. She hugged him back, feeling the love pour from him to her as a gentle, yet loving father would his child. When he pulled back from her, he just stared at her. There was a twinkle there that wasn't before. She supposed it was the knowledge that he could hold his own children whenever he wanted.

"We're going to beat this, my girl. I just know it." She nodded and he laughed. "Yes, sir, we are going to beat this thing and live a long and happy life right here on the farm."

He walked away with Jed and Zak, the three of them talking a mile a minute. As the others dispersed, each of them saying they had to work on a plan to take care of the chamber, it left her and Asher alone in the field. Essie was suddenly embarrassed to be alone with him.

"Have I told you lately how much I love you?" She shook her head. "I do. Very much so. And I think you are the most amazing person I've ever met. And for me, that is a lot of people."

"You're very old." He nodded. "I worry about you sometimes. You might fall and break a hip. Or worse, you might just keel over one day, and where will I be?"

"Where indeed." He pulled her to him and kissed her. "I want you. Right now, out here in the grass."

"I'd like that as well." He lifted her up by her ass, and she wrapped her legs around his waist. "Where are we going?"

"Close. I don't think I can wait long to have you." He kissed her twice more as they moved, stopping only long enough for him to strip another article of clothing off one or both of them. By the time they were deep within the trees, she had nothing on but her panties, and they were badly torn and he was down to his socks. She nearly screamed when he took them in a deep body of water.

"I forgot about this until the other day. We used to come here as kids. Dad would fish upstream and we'd make enough racket down here to wake the dead." He took them deeper until her breasts were just above the water. "I want to make love to you here, but I need to cool off a little first. Otherwise, I'm going to take you hard and quick, and it's doubtful you'll get much out of it."

"Oh you don't have to worry about that. I'm going to get my pleasure even if I have to give it to myself." His eyes darkened. "Asher, would you like to see me masturbate?"

He pulled them to the edge of the water and laid her so that her body was just under it. She ran her fingers down her body while he watched her, never taking his eyes off her trailing hand. He fisted his cock in slow strong strokes, and she knew that when she came, he was going to come all over her.

Sliding her fingers under what was left of her panties, she moaned when she touched her clit. Asher went to his knees then, still holding his cock as he pulled her panties off her body. His hand was moving faster over his hard shaft even as precum started to stream from the tip.

"Tell me what you're doing, how you're feeling." She nodded and touched her clit again. It was the most erotic thing she'd ever felt, having him watch her as she played with herself. "Tell me, Essie. Tell me what you're doing."

"My pussy is wet and hot." She stroked her nether lips and moaned again. "My hard clit is sticking beyond my lips, just waiting for me to tease it. I love the way it feels under my fingers. Hard and ready; each time I touch it, shivers run through my body."

"I want to come on you. Shoot my cum all over your pretty body, then eat you until you come down my throat." She opened her legs, and he leaned forward. "Show me."

Using her other hand, she spread her lips for him. He watched her, his hand moving over his cock faster and faster as she fingered herself. Sliding her finger into her slit, she nearly came up off the ground when she touched the spot. As she did it again and again, she pinched her clit hard enough to toss her over the edge.

Asher cried out. Leaning back on his knees, his cum shot out of his cock in a high arch and landed on her in hot jets of cream. She screamed then; another climax from just his cum on her touched off two more powerful and satisfying releases. But then he leaned down and sucked her clit into his mouth as he pressed his fingers into her, both her ass and her pussy.

"Come for me." She told him she couldn't. "You can. Come for me and let me drink from you."

He lifted her body up so that only her shoulders were on the ground. He was eating her, watching her as he did it, and she begged him to give her what she needed. When he bit her, his teeth seemingly taking a piece out of her pussy, she cried out, her entire body coming for him to the point where she saw stars behind her lids.

He let her down then, only to pick her up and slide his cock into her as he sat on the edge of the water. Laying them down, her back on the shoreline, he fucked her hard, taking her over the edge twice more as he pounded her hard. When he came his body bowed back and stiffened, and she would swear that she felt each drop of his cum as he emptied in her.

Exhaustion took her then. Not like she lay down to nap, but like it was a freight train running her down and taking her under.

Chapter 10

"I serve only you." If he said that once more Helena was going to kill him and have Robarts go and get her another body to use in the coven. She'd told him five times already that she was just his master in this, and that he would serve the whole not her alone. As it was, this was the fifth man he'd brought to her to see if he'd work.

"Robarts?" The man came running to her, his head bowed down. "Take him to the chambers and see if you can get him to clean up the mess. Dusting and stuff like that."

"Yes, mistress." He took the man with him and she sat down. She'd done a little trading in town and looked around at the things she'd been able to get. She knew that the dead were never going to tell that she'd robbed them, but hell, it did look really nice in her little house.

Frowning, she thought about the little town she'd been to. It had been decades since she'd been there. Had any reason to be there, she supposed. But things had changed a great deal in that time. The merchandise store was gone and replaced with a place that advertised that everything in it was a dollar. And even at that price it seemed like she was being robbed.

Then there was the bank. Four of them were there now when there had been only the one, and it wasn't one that she'd ever been in. But the little shop that she'd wanted, the one that had always come through when she was down on her luck, was gone altogether. There wasn't even a building there any longer. She knew this because she'd gone around the block several times to see if she'd been lost somehow. But in her search she had found the little shop in the alley off the main road. There she was able to get all her needs and then some. The Little Palace of Goods certainly lived up to its name. The only issue she'd had was the lack of cash or credit card, whatever that was.

So she'd come back to the house to see what she had to trade. The girl behind the counter, Mystic her name had been, never said she'd not trade her, so Helena was counting on the trade and not cash. But it had done her little good either way as she'd had nothing there of value. But she knew where there was gold.

It had taken Helena an hour to get the things she thought might bring her a penny. The chain around the king's neck was something that she'd always coveted, and it was the first thing she put into her sack. Then there was the jewels, all of them scattered around the table for the guests to take when they left for their home. She had picked up all of those as she made her way back up the table to the lord, the man to the right of Ruben.

She knew the man to be a thief. Actually, most of the men and women at the table would steal the pennies from a dead man's eyes if they thought no one was looking. But when she went through his pockets, she found not only a hand full of the gems but a necklace that she fell in love with. Helena had kept it for herself.

Mystic had been a little reluctant to take the gems, not that she blamed her much. Where would she sell them if there was no merchant to trade with in town? But after a bit she'd told her that she'd take one of the white diamonds for a hundred dollars' worth of items. Eight of the fist-sized diamonds and a few other gems got her all that she wanted.

It had taken her two trips from her cart to the house to get all the things in the house. Then another hour to take the stuff that would be used for the ritual to the cave. There had been a cave in at some time since she'd been gone, and she had to have the coven remove the larger stones so that she was able to get through. By the time she'd finished setting up the chamber, she'd ended up sleeping on the dais for a few hours just to make it back home. Robarts had watched over her.

Helena got up and looked around at her new things. Some of them were as useless as a man for the most part, but they were pretty. The glass jars in the window, all in varying shades of blue, sparkled sunlight into the room, and it danced along the walls and floors. She admired the blue candles she'd gotten, all of them a different scent. She wanted to light one of them, burn it now to see if it smelled as good burning as it did just sitting on the pottery plate that she'd gotten, but didn't want to have to use it up just yet. Helena decided that she was going to buy a lot of them once she had the funds.

"Not that I really need them, but I deserve them." She was talking to herself again, a trait that she'd tried to break herself of a long time ago. The herbs now hanging from her ceiling weren't the best of quality, but they would do for now. She had seeds too, things she was going to plant as soon as she got this business with the dragons over with.

"Perhaps I'll hire someone to do it." She'd have enough money, she knew that. Six dragons would bring a nice purse to her. Excitement coursed through her body until she had to dance a little just to dispel it. She was going to be so rich.

Money really didn't mean that much to her. It was the things that she could get with it that really appealed to her. The little touches that she could add to her house. The new rocker on her porch, and she was very excited to see what she could do with the coffee beans that she'd purchased. The girl had been no help with that now that she'd remembered.

Helena had to ask her three times how she planted them. They smelled rich and full of a darkness that she could only think was from evil. But Mystic had only stared at her when she'd asked her the third time how to plant then, then she'd laughed so hard that Helena left the store without any knowledge to make them grow.

"Stupid chit." Then there were the things that Helena had left alone. There were large jars of eye of newt and bat wings. She was still trying to figure out why anyone would pay for such items when they were free for the taking. And they smelled funny, like something had died on them before they'd actually died. Shaking her head, she didn't understand a great many things in the new town, and decided that other than going back to the Palace, she would stay away from the little town.

Helena knew it was time to call the coven together and tell them of her plan. Robarts knew some of it; he'd had to go after the thirteenth man, so she'd had to tell him something. But she didn't share that there were six dragons and not just the one. She was still working out where to store their bodies once she killed them.

It was a problem that was, compared to the other things she was working out, small. There was the food to feed the king and his court, someone to cook it, and how to bring the man with the dragons to her. That was the problem.

Helena thought about the woman. She would be the easiest to capture being a mere human and all, but she still had to get onto the property and get her. Then figure out how to contact the man so that he'd come to get the girl, and she'd capture him then. It made her head spin just thinking about it.

As she made her way to the mouth of the chamber, she watched as the floors were being scrubbed and the walls wiped down. A great many webs had made their way into this room, and she had spent the better part of yesterday after she'd returned just gathering them in her basket. She now had a near endless supply of them for her spells.

"Mistress, we have been cleaning the dishes in the dining area, but we have run into...there is something that you must see." She asked him what it was, and he motioned for her to follow.

"I don't have time for your games, Robarts. Just tell me." He told her that he could not read, that she should see it. "Oh, all right."

It was more than likely something that had been there for decades or more, and no one had noticed it before. She thought of the night that Anthony had come into the chamber, just appearing there as if he'd known about it the entire time. Ruben had been so pissed at her that he'd slapped her enough to bruise her head for a week after. But Anthony had said some things that had her pause in her steps as she remembered them.

"I will return one day and destroy all that you have built." Ruben had laughed. He knew that the stone walls would never come down and that Anthony was full of himself. "Mark my words. Someday this will lay in ruin and your body will have its final resting place along with all your court."

He'd been right about that, she supposed. The chamber had been the final resting place for them all, but Anthony's walls had come down long before and her own chamber still stood. She was smiling when she entered the room, and froze when she saw what Robarts was talking about.

In large letters that were too big to ever be missed, it said, "I have returned." The letters were in a fine script, one that made Helena believe that it had been done by an educated man rather than the idiots now standing and staring at it. She looked at Robarts when he cleared his throat, and she went to where he now pointed. Like a lifeless dummy, she went to area and staggered at the message there.

There was a dragon painted on the floor. It was a good rendition of the one she'd seen just recently, but this one had his claws digging into what looked like a lake of blood. When she stepped closer, looking at what he held there, she could see herself, her face staring right back at her as the dragon held her in his sharp claws. The words there were no less scary in that they said. "You will die soon."

"Scrub it away. Both of them. I want them gone." Robarts told her that he had tried. "Well, try harder. I don't know which one of you did this, but I will find out."

She left the dining room, vowing never to enter it again. Whoever had done this was going to pay dearly. She moved to the dais and held onto it as she tried to think what had happened, who had been down here and why. And she wasn't sure, but she had a feeling that whatever it was written in, it would never be scrubbed away.

And she knew…just knew…who had put it there. It was the king, Anthony, and he was indeed returning for her. Something touched her on the arm. She had no idea what, but it caused her to turn and scream, her power tossing the person who had dared touch her across the room. When she was over her fright, she looked at the man who was dead, his head split open and his brain spilling out onto the floor. She had just killed Robarts.

~~~

Asher wanted to get things over with. It was putting a strain on all of them just wondering what they needed to do to get rid of the witch, her magic that she was hanging over the rest of their lives. He walked along the streets in the town looking for the disturbance that Essie had told him about today.

"I don't see anything. Is she sure that it was around here?" Asher told Gideon she was positive. "Okay. But all that's around here is a defunked pizza place and a shop that sells shit to wannabes."

"Wanna be what?" Gideon told him it was some sort of candle shop. "We'd better look. That way we can tell her that we checked everything."

As soon as he stood outside the shop, he knew that it was the place. It nearly vibrated with energy, and he was pretty sure that it wasn't coming from all the neon that was flashing in the windows. He reached out to touch the door knob when he felt Essie touch his mind.

Don't. He pulled his hand back as if he'd been burned. *That's it. I don't know what you're going to do, but don't…whatever it was.*

I was going to go inside and see what is there. She didn't answer him, so he continued. *Gideon is with me. He and I are going in together. And I have Kiaran with me.*

Can he be a man there? He told her he didn't think so. *I wish that he could…have him ready if you go in. I'm not saying you have to, but be ready for anything.*

He opened the door carefully and stepped inside the Little Palace of Goods. Asher felt Kiaran stir, but he didn't move from his body. As soon as he was over the threshold, everything that had felt evil on the outside seemed to disappear. And the woman behind the counter looked like she might have felt something as well.

"You bring that bad vibe with you?" He shook his head at the large woman behind the cash register. "Coming from somewhere. I had me a spell out there, so I know you don't mean me no harm, but something was there."

"My wife…she felt something as well." She stared at him, then nodded as he continued. "She said that she knew something had happened here, and she sent us to find out what it was. My brother and I."

"She's a white witch then?" Asher said she was more of a supernatural than a witch, and the woman nodded. "Gobi is my name. I'm a white witch myself. But I sell to whoever has the coin. You bringing me business or asking me questions? Cause I have a few of my own."

"I was wondering about a woman who might have been in recently. She would have been completely out of place, and might have asked you for some odd items." Gobi didn't move, not even to shake her head. "She's about five foot six or so, tiny little thing with dark hair. She has a sort of cracked voice."

"All but the dark hair, she's been here. I didn't wait on her, but my assistant did. Who, I might as well tell you, is gone. She left me a few things that she said the woman paid with, then said she was taking the rest. Took me an hour to figure out it was all real."

"What was it?" She didn't answer him but went through the beaded curtain to the back. When she returned, she laid out a small money bag on the counter and told him to come see.

"She didn't have any money, Melody told me. She don't go by that here. She calls herself Mystic, of all things. Anyway, she left me this note telling me that this woman came in to buy some stuff, and she didn't have any cash. Didn't seem to know what a credit card was either. Then when she left, Melody thought she'd not be back. Then an hour or so later she comes in with these things." She dumped the bag out, and there were four of the biggest diamonds Asher had ever seen, along with a few rubies and about a dozen smaller emeralds. "Don't know how much she took with her when she left, but she said it was only a few of the pieces. I'm supposing she took the diamonds. When I looked over the surveillance tapes, I could see there were more than just this few of them."

"How much merchandise did she take?" Asher was too busy calculating the amount of money that was left behind when Gideon asked his question. "I mean, you're well stocked, and I'm assuming since the woman had no sense of money, Mystic or whatever her name is would have taken advantage of that."

"She wrote it all down." The sales page was handed to Gideon, and he handed it to Asher. There were things on the page she'd need for a spell, he supposed, but there were things on the list that he knew had nothing at all to do with whatever she was planning.

"She bought some candles. Six of them. Do they have any special properties?" The woman shook her head and told him they were just smelly ones. "And this…what is an ackron?"

Her cackle of a laugh had Asher smile. "Had to figure that one out myself. She never was any good at writing. Maybe if she took enough diamonds with her, she can find someone to teach her a thing or two. It's apron. It's the only thing on the list that is not accounted for. I had me four of them and now I only have three." Asher asked her what was special about it. "Had a spell written on it. Not a real one, but a joke of a one. I had me a good laugh at it when I read it the first time. Asked you to gather this stuff up that would summon someone to you. Won't work, but it's got a lot to things on it that I sell. And yeah, before you ask, she got a few of them on it. I'm thinking she's wanting herself a man and she thinks to lure him to her bed."

"What did it say to have?" Asher was laughing with Gobi when she was still giggling. "It must be really good."

"Oh it is. But only if you can read Latin." Asher told her that he could. "Good. *Amphora vini Lorem gens naris lucernis et equis satis fune ligabis eum lamina si necesse sit.*"

Asher did laugh then. He turned to Gideon when he asked what it said. "Bottle of wine, sexy nighty, scented candles, pretty plate to serve on, and a rope to tie him up if need be. I'm thinking she'll need a good strong rope to keep this person with her."

When they finished the business with Helena, he purchased a few things for Caroline. Gobi even provided them with a picture she'd captured from the cameras, and also gave Asher one of the diamonds. He told her he'd return it, but he thought that Essie, with her new powers, could use it as a scribe.

As it turned out, Gobi knew who she was and had told him that she'd had her eye on a few things for a while now. He got the list of things that Caroline wanted as a gift to the witch, and told Gobi that if Caroline ever needed anything to send him the bill.

"That's mighty generous of you." Asher told Gobi that Caroline was a good friend and she nodded. "I might be able to...let me make a call for a minute. I want to check something."

"Where do you suppose she got the gems?" Gideon told him he had no idea, and Asher thought of the chamber he'd visited with Essie. "I think she robbed the dead. I mean, the king and a few of his court were in the dining area when I was there with Essie. She might have went there when she needed the cash."

"If that's the case then she's just broken her own spell." Asher asked his brother what he meant. "There is a golden rule about keeping things the same. I don't have a clue where it originated from, but I think people in sports sort of run with that one. You know, the same socks, the same bat, or whatever. Like you when you have a meeting with some clients...you wear the same tie." Asher nodded.

"I think we all do it to some point." Gideon nodded. "Okay, so she's robbed from the dead and used it to purchase things for the ritual to kill a dragon. How is that breaking her spell?"

"Ah, but she didn't just buy things for the ritual, now did she? She used it for her own personal gain. And that, my dear brother, is going to get us into the chamber easier than I thought."

They looked up when Gobi laughed.

"You got yourself a right smart brother there, Mr. Asher." Asher nodded, but before he could thank her, she continued. "I just summoned me a few answers for you. There's been a rash of bodies turning up at the morgue, and a few of them have come up missing. I'm thinking that your witch is getting her coven back up. And if she's looking for dragons, she'll need thirteen of them."

Asher knew that in the back of his mind, and it wasn't until she asked him what the thirteen meant to him that he remembered Essie telling him that there had been thirteen tombs, but the body in one of them was actually crushed. He started to tell Gobi that when something else occurred to him.

"I was born thirteen months, thirteen days, thirteen hours, and thirteen minutes before my brother. And we were all the same down the line." She nodded and started writing things down. Asking him what else. "There are twelve of us, so that—"

"Thirteen of us. Essie makes us thirteen." Asher nodded when Gideon corrected him. When Gobi laughed, he looked at her. She handed him a sheet of paper with some words written on it.

"Go tell Caroline that you need her to put this together for you. She'll know what it is. By damn, I wish I could be there when this happens. Thirteen of you. Damn, what a fine coven you have of your own. Do you...? No, I can see that you have no idea. That's fine. She'll know." She laughed again, and he could see that she was really enjoying this. "I'm going to give you what you need to take to her."

After about another hour of Gobi laughing and joking about how Caroline was the luckiest woman in the world and so on, Asher and Gideon left the Palace. He didn't have a clue what was going on, but he was excited to know that someone thought they could win. Asher didn't exactly have his doubts, but he was really worried. Every time he thought of the dream, he'd get chills. Because in his mind, he still saw Essie there.

Chapter 11

Screaming would get her nowhere, but she was thinking it might release some of the pressure that was building up. Helena watched the man she'd brought to replace Robarts and wanted to kill him again. It had exhausted her, bringing back two men in the same week, and this one was proving to be a total waste of her previous energy.

"You have to say it right or it's not going to work." He nodded at her and smiled. He'd been doing that since she'd woken him. "Say it again. This time make the words work for you, not against you."

The grin was what she hated the most. What she wanted to know was how the hell was someone supposed to know a simpleton was going to wake when you rose the dead? Then there was the added fact that no matter how many times she'd told him to wear his robe in the chamber, he wanted to show up naked. Naked of all things.

His dick was hard all the time too. She'd been tempted on more than on occasion to walk up to him and have him fuck her. But she was afraid that she'd have to walk him through each step, and that wouldn't be fun.

As he mumbled through the words again, she looked at him. Christ, she'd done well to pick a nice, healthy member. His body looked as if it had been sculpted from stone, and his bare chest, even of any hair, made her want to lick him. When he stood up and pressed his cock to her, she lay back on the table she was sitting on.

She wore nothing beneath her robe, and he had her exposed before she could think to tell him to be careful with it. His cock slammed deep inside of her, and she cried out with the pleasure of a dick so deep. He was thick, she'd known that, but he filled her like she'd never been filled before. Cupping her own breasts, she offered him one, and he sucked it hard enough that she was sure he was looking for something more. When he bit her, drawing blood, she cried out her release even as he pounded her harder.

A dick at her mouth made her open for it. She looked up to see one of the other men at her head, and took his cock into her. He wasn't nearly as thick or long as the man between her thighs, but he was fucking her mouth like her pussy was being pounded.

Her breasts were exposed more, her robe pulled away. There were so many hands on her that she came three times before she realized that there were four more touching her. The men at her breasts, one at each of them, were holding their stiff cocks while they suckled. The dick in her mouth filled her throat even as the cock in her pussy released as well. Cum spread over her; hands were smoothing it over her skin like a lotion, a hot sticky cream.

They moved around her, each of them taking turns where the other had been. She felt glorious; her body felt worshiped as they fucked and sucked at her. Helena moaned when she was lifted up, then turned and bent over the table. The cock there, the one that had fucked her first, looked like a feast for her, and she took him into her mouth even as someone spread her legs and ate her from beneath. Then a cock entered her ass and she screamed out with the pain even as she was coming again and again.

The men changed, and her position on the table did as well. She was fucked hard sometimes and then gently the next. Her pussy was sore but felt good; her breasts were bruised but well loved. She lay there when they'd all come on her and inside of her, basking in the pure joy of so many releases. Looking up when a cock slowly entered her, she watched the first man fuck her again, his body swaying to the motion of the man at his ass.

She knew that they'd been pleasuring each other as they did her. Helena didn't care so long as they never left her without a partner. The man at his ass lifted her legs up to the shoulders of the man in front of her, and she felt him go deeper still. It was a slow easy fuck that made her come twice, a soft climax that made her want more.

The cum on her breasts gave her hands something to slide with. She pinched her nipples hard as she enjoyed the men. When he grunted and leaned over her, he took her breast into his mouth as the second man fucked him hard enough to have her moved across the table. When he came, shouting out his release, both she and the man fucking her did as well. They both dropped on her, and Helena closed her eyes.

Helena had a great deal to do. But the soft afterglow of coming was making her so relaxed that she let sleep take her. She'd get up in a few minutes, she'd told herself, even as her body fell slowly into the abyss that was sleep. Yawning once, a man curled his body around hers, and she snuggled into it thinking that she might keep him if he did this every night. Maybe all of them.

It was dark in the chamber when she woke. Helena knew it was late because the fire had burned down to just a few embers...enough to keep the room tolerable but not warm. She was glad that someone had put her robe over her. Sitting up, she realized two things almost at once. She was alone in the big room, and someone was in the dining area.

"I told you to keep out of there." Pulling her robe around her body, she moved across the room. "Just because it was a good fuck, it does not leave you to do as you —"

"Hello, Helena the Black." She stared at the man standing there and staggered back a step. "Oh, you don't want to leave me now. We've only just started talking again. Have you enjoyed...? Well, I guess you have been enjoying yourself. Those men, they fucked you over well?"

Ruben was standing there as if he'd not been dead these thousands of years. Swallowing three times before she could answer him, she looked at his body still lying in the chair. As he moved to it, she started to leave, but he snapped his fingers and she was bound to the wall.

"You're dead." He nodded and smiled at her. She saw the bug come from his mouth to his ear, and she shivered. Nothing about this was good; she knew this deep in her bones. "What are you doing here? I...I have been keeping you safe."

"But not from Manchester. Oh, I know that he fucked you while I lay in here dying. I saw him coming deep within that pussy of yours while I tried to fight for life. Did you not care, Helena the Black, that your lover in here was being murdered?"

"He tried to blame me, but I had nothing to do with it." Ruben moved toward her, and she could see that he wasn't nearly as well-kempt as he'd looked when she'd first seen him. There were bones showing on his hands. His legs were bare from the holes in his pants that showed raw muscle where there should have been nothing but bones. "How are you here? I thought you long dead."

"I'm well aware that I should be dust. But the mountain has kept me like this." He turned right, then left, for her, and she remembered that he would preen whenever he could. "Do you not find me to be as sexy as I was? I assure you, if you keep fucking those men, I will be."

"What do you mean?" But she knew. It was magic. The dead were fucking her, and she only just realized it. It mattered little that they were whole, unlike the man in front of her. They were using her up, her magic, by fucking the queen of their coven. "You're making them do this."

"Of course I am. And why not? I should like to be around for a long time. And you're going to help me." Another snap of his fingers brought her simpleton to her. He was hard again, his cock dripping at the tip like he'd been waiting and thinking of her. "He's going to bring you over and over, and by the time you are drained, I will be whole."

Her robe was opened, and no matter how hard she tried to keep her legs together, she couldn't. Even as she shoved at the man with her feet, knocking him to the floor, two more men came in and held her legs open while he fucked her.

Ruben came to stand next to her and watch. "Do you not love the sight of a dick all wet with a woman's cream? It makes the fucking easier. You're going to come soon, and when you do, someone else will hold you while you are fucked again and again."

"Please, don't do this. I worshiped you. Did all your bidding." He laughed at her and ran his fingers over the dick going in and out of her. "Ruben, please."

The slap at her face had her screaming out her release. She came twice more before she could ask why he'd hit her. As her binding kept her to the wall, the men's hands at her legs widened her more. Then Ruben was there; his dick, nearly rotted off, was at her entrance.

"My turn. And you will not call me Ruben again. I am King to you." His cock slammed into her and she screamed.

Helena sat up on the dais and screamed again. A dream. It had been a dream. Just to be sure, she stood up and checked her body. There was still the cum on her, but none of it was fresh. The fire had died down but the room was cold now, her breath showing as she panted. Running to the dining chamber, she was relieved to see that nothing was out of place here. But as she moved toward the head, where Ruben was, she slowed her steps. Staring at him, she couldn't figure out what it was until the bug went from his ear to near his mouth, and Ruben's tongue came out and captured it, taking it into his mouth.

Trying to escape the horrific nightmare, she turned and ran. The wall seemed to come out of nowhere and she slammed against it, hitting her head and knocking herself out. She fell to the floor thinking that she'd made a terrible mistake, but had not a clue what it was.

~~~

Essie lay back on the grass. Magic was exhausting, she'd come to realize. Glancing over at Caroline, who had a huge smile on her face, she wondered how she felt. When she looked at her, Essie could see the line of exhaustion on her face.

"You'll get stronger as you get more practice. Today was different because we had to make things so real." She nodded, not sure what to say to what they'd done to Helena. "It was good that you knew so much. It helped us make her believe us."

"You're welcome, but I still don't know how making her think Ruben is alive is going to help us. I mean, it's fun and all, but to what end?" Caroline sat up, and so did Essie. The others were there, all six of the men and the dragons that belonged to them. They had formed a circle around them, her mostly, to add to their magic. When she realized that Caroline had not answered her, she looked at her again. "Are you okay?"

"Oh yes. I've not had this much fun in a very long time. But at the same time, I'm old, and it takes a lot out of a witch to do what will come naturally to you." Before she could say anything, not even sure what to say, Caroline continued. "In answer to your question, having her think that someone is watching over her, even a dead man, is going to keep her energy level low. I mean, if you thought that every time you closed your eyes some man, a long dead man, was going to come to you and threaten you, what would you do? Not sleep. And she's going to need her energy levels to be high to try and take you on."

"Everyone has this confidence in me that I don't feel. It's kind of scary how…I don't have a clue what I'm doing." Caroline nodded and said nothing. "And you do that a lot. Like you think if you wait long enough I'll get it. But I don't. I'm just a person who just happens to have all this extra shit that I don't have any idea how to use."

"No, but you're learning." Asher came to sit behind her, and she leaned into his big body. It was both comforting and rejuvenating at the same time. She looked at Caroline when she laughed.

"You drive me nutty, did you know that?" Caroline laughed and lay back on the grass. All of them were a little on the nutty side, but she was getting used to it. Except for the witch. She thought…well, Essie wasn't sure what she thought most of the time, but she did scare her a little.

"She's just as afraid of you." Looking over her shoulder at Asher when he spoke, she asked him how that was even possible. "Let me show you. No. It would be easier if you showed me. Think of the day you grew the tree in the yard. Do you remember it?"

"Yes. The ground told me to do it. They said that if I hadn't helped it, it would have died the next time the man came to mow the yard. He hates trimming around the trees and such." He laughed, and she glared at him. "Are you going to explain this or make fun of me?"

"Both. But for now, I'm going to explain. Okay, the tree would have died. Did the grounds tell you that the man hated trimming, or did something else?" She started to ask him where else she would have known that from when he told her to think. "You know where you got the information; just tell me."

She looked at the tree in question. It was swaying back and forth, and she felt it calm her, the movement comforting like when Asher put his arms around her. Closing her eyes, she thought about the ground and the woman who had spoken to her. Suddenly, there she was, only this time she could actually see her.

"She's here." She felt Asher hold her tighter and knew that he was entering her mind to look too. "She's…wow, she's beautiful."

The woman bowed and then smiled at her. Essie felt herself leave her body somehow, and found herself standing next to the woman. Asher was there as well, but he was sitting on the grass away from them.

"He'll hear us but not be able to engage." Essie nodded. "You have summoned me at a perfect time, Lady Esmerelda. I have a lesson for you."

"I have enough to keep straight now, thanks. But I would like to know the answer to Asher's question. How did I know?" The woman nodded and looked behind her. Essie did as well. The grass was there, then the trees. As the house came into view, so did a man on a lawn mower with a truck in the background. She watched as he mowed the lawn, running over some small flowers and a few saplings.

"You felt their loss, did you not?" Essie nodded. She had. When she's put her feet into the dirt, the sorrow of their death had touched her. "You know because he tells the plants and such here that he does not want them in the yard. The same way that the mountain spoke to you about his pain, and the way the lakes will tell you of their problems, their concerns. You are an elemental faerie, Lady Esmerelda, a queen in your own right."

The touch to her arm was soft, almost like a kitten's breath. When the woman stepped back, the scene she'd created disappeared and she was standing in an open field. Essie looked around and knew this place. The woman followed her when she went to the edge of the mountain and found the opening of the small hut that she'd been born in.

"She still lives here?" The woman nodded. "Why? I mean, she had so much when I lived here. Money out the ass, jewels that she'd stolen off the people she...we killed."

"Money means as little to her as the men and women that she has killed. It runs through her fingers and pockets, like it is water from yonder lake. She knows not the meaning of keeping for a rainy day; the concept of getting things that will keep her warm and safe are not a part of her thoughts when she has money to line her wallet. She will forever be on the verge of being broke or near starvation. She will never be anything more than she is right now." Essie could see that.

"When I left here I was shocked by the difference in our lives and those of the people nearby. It was as if she'd shut herself off from anything modern and things that would have made our lives so much better. She was…I didn't even know what indoor plumbing was, or electricity. It was as if she'd been born in a time where there was only what she has now, and she'd never made her way to come into this century." The woman nodded, and Essie looked where she knew there were graves. "All those lives lost, and for what gain? None. I helped her kill those people, and for that I will forever be guilty."

"You did nothing to expedite their deaths, Lady Esmerelda. You were but a pawn in the larger picture of things. You may have thought yourself alone, but you were not. The food provided for you, the earth, our earth, gave to you. Once you were able to move beyond the doors of the house we helped you more, and you, in return, helped us. Do you not remember that?" Essie started to shake her head but stopped to think.

"I planted this tree. I mean, the seeds that were from the apple that was…that I'm assuming you gave to me." She nodded and smiled, the brightness of it making her warmer. "There were other seeds as well. A pear and a melon. Sometimes I had no idea what the things were that I was eating, but I planted what I couldn't eat."

"You did. And now the earth is rich with plants just ready to burst forward. Many of them are long since gone, their only life in the seeds that you planted." Essie went to the tree, full now with apples, and reached up to touch one. It fell into her hand as if she'd pulled it free. "It's giving back to you in hopes that you will plant more."

"How does this answer my question?" Essie smelled the fruit before putting it into her pocket to save for later. "I mean, who am I that makes me so special?"

"You are the queen of the dragons, my dear. As Asher is the king. It was written many years ago that a king and queen of great power would come to us and save us all. You are that woman. And the love that you have for Asher makes your blood, your bond with me stronger." She asked her who she was. "Why, I'm the lady of the earth, such as you are the queen. I am here to serve you and to help you when you should desire my help."

"You can help me take the witch of the mountain on and keep the others safe?" The lady nodded. "Then I want you to show me how. I want you to give me all the information you have on me, and what I can do to use the powers that I have."

"It will be my pleasure to serve you, my lady." It was too late; Essie knew it as soon as the lady's hand touched her. The power surged through her in such a way that she felt as if she had put her wet feet in an electrical socket. Then when she thought it was finished, her body bruised inside and out, she was lifted from the earth and something else touched her. Essie couldn't speak, couldn't scream when it became too much. As she was gently laid back to the earth, she noticed that Asher was beside her. "You will need to rest now. There is much to come as yet, and you will need your strength."

Essie nodded and closed her eyes. A hand touched hers and she knew it was Asher. When someone else curled his fingers around hers, she looked over at Kiaran and smiled. Whatever the hell had just happened, they all got it.

"The next time someone offers to give you something powerful like that, could you please warn me?" She nodded at Kiaran and looked over at Asher when he laughed.

"That was fucking amazing, but I'm exhausted." She was too, and closed her eyes again. "We'll deal with this later, okay?"

"Yes." Essie felt the darkness swallow her up. It was gentle in the way that she knew she'd be safe, but it was consuming all the same. As she let her body drift off to sleep, she thought of something else but didn't voice it. But the woman laughed a little, and she knew that she'd heard her.

"I will take care of it, my lady. Immediately." Essie thanked her and let sleep roll over her. She thought that she'd told her that she loved her, but Essie was too sleepy to ask her to repeat herself. Rest. Once she rested, she'd ask her then. The twinkling sound of laughter made her frown, but this too took more effort than she wanted to expend to ask her about.

Chapter 12

Asher woke hard as stone. His need to take Essie was making him salivate, and he reached for her. Her body came to his as if he'd summoned her, and she was gloriously naked. And so was he.

"Ride me." She settled over his lap in seconds. Her nipples were as hard as his cock, and he leaned up when she sat over his hips and suckled at one while she rode his body. He wanted to be inside of her, having her riding him while he fucked her, but she was holding his cock to her pussy and he knew she was going to come without him.

Her release had him pulling her tighter to him. She cried out, her body still rocking against his, as he rolled her to her back. Moving down her body, Asher nipped at her hot skin and then kissed the wound only to do it again lower, making his way to her pussy. When he touched his tongue to her navel, sucking on the indentation until she begged him to take her, Asher looked up at her and fisted his cock.

"I don't know which I want to do more, fuck you or eat you." She told him both. "My pleasure."

Not wanting to miss a drop of her hot cream, he buried his mouth over her clit and sucked hard. She came, screaming out his name even as she flooded his mouth. Drinking her down, lapping as much of it into his mouth as he could, Asher slid his fingers into her and fucked her like he wanted to do with his cock. As she came again, then again, he knew that if he waited much longer, he was going to come himself.

Moving up her body, he took her breast into his mouth. They were lovely and probably the sexiest part of her as far as he was concerned. Then there was her pussy. He didn't want to forget that. But as he moved up her, taking her mouth with his, he decided that there was nothing about her that wasn't his favorite part of her. Sliding his cock into her, he lifted his body from hers as he moved in and out of her.

"I love the way you feel wrapped all around me." Nodding, she put her legs up around his hips and he slid deeper. "That's it, baby, take me. Christ, you have no idea how much I want to come inside of you. But I need to bring you again."

"Asher, as soon as you come, I'm going to scream again and come too." He fucked her harder, his cock seeming to have a mind of its own. "Please. More, I need more."

Not one to disappoint his wife, he took her harder, using some of his strength, some of his magic to bring her again and again. When she begged him to stop, she had nothing left, Asher used the last push of his magic to bring her again, and he came roaring out her name.

Asher tried not to simply drop on top of her, but he was drained. He did roll to his back, bringing her with him at the last moment so as not to crush her. He looked up at the sky when he could manage to open his eyes finally. She was looking at him with her chin on her fist.

"I love you." Smiling, he told her he loved her as well. "I mean, I really love you. Not that 'damn that was a good fuck, I love you for it,' love, but a serious I am in love with you."

He was at a loss for words and pulled her to him for a long, consuming kiss. "I love you so much that I have no idea how to express it to you."

Nodding, she laid her head on his chest as she spoke. "The lady of the earth, she gave us some powerful shit. I think maybe Kiaran got it as well."

"He did. I think he's a little overwhelmed by it as well." He felt her nod. "What do you suppose we're supposed to do with it? I mean…really, I have no idea what we got, but it was a lot of power and information."

"I think…." She lifted her head up again and looked at him. "This thing with us being the king and queen of dragons, I think she gave us what we'll need to deal with that too."

"Yes." He lifted his hand from her back and looked at his arm. There was a mark there that had never been there before, and before he could ask her about it, Essie answered his unspoken question.

"I have one too. It's just like the one on Kiaran. But ours are gold and his is silver." Asher remembered it now and put his hand back to rubbing her back. "Asher? I want to get this thing over with concerning Helena. I don't want to be there making her have sex again."

Asher laughed and she did too. "I can imagine that it would be weird. But as Caroline said, it was necessary to make her unfocused."

"I know." She sat up then and reached for the pants and shirt that was lying next to a pile for him. "Someone thought of us being naked. And so you know, I'm sort of disconcerted that we're forever in this state of undress in the open."

He watched her dress, thinking that he would have her naked all the time if he could, but she had a point. There were his brothers here as well as his dad now, and Elbert. When she told him she was going to the house, he told her he'd be along shortly. A nap sounded really good, and he had no qualms like she did of doing so naked.

Closing his eyes, he felt his body, already sated and relaxed, start to slip under the spell of sleep. But before he could get into the deeper part of it, a shadow fell across his face and he smiled.

"Come back to play some more? I have to tell you, you've sort of worn me out." When Essie didn't answer, he opened one eye and tried to focus on her. But the sun was too bright, and she was in shadows. Before he could say anything else, the pain in his head exploded, and he saw who it was.

I'm hurt. Helena has me. It was all he could send out before darkness, painful black inky darkness, took him under.

~~~

Kiaran staggered under the pain. He grabbed for something to keep him upright and pulled Essie and his brother Zak down with him. The pain, the sickening pain, made him reach for his head, thinking that something had driven a pike through it.

I'm hurt. Helena has me, echoed into his head over and over. Sitting as still as he could so as not to hurt any more, he reached for his other half, only to hit a hard wall. When something was shoved into his hand, then pushed to his mouth, he drank it. The harsh liquid of alcohol stripped the pain in his head with its surprise taste. As he coughed, trying to catch his breath, he realized that Essie was sitting beside him, and that she knew what had happened.

"We'll get him from her. Now." Essie nodded, but she looked…well, she looked as pained as he felt. "Honey, he's not going to die. Not so long as we're here to get him back. You have to believe me."

"She hurt him." He nodded and had to hold his head to stop the pain. "She hurt you too. I didn't know that would happen."

"It's never happened before. I have felt his pain in a sort of soft way, but nothing like this." Zak handed him a glass of juice, something he wished he'd had the first time. Drinking it down, he felt marginally better but not completely healed. He could only imagine what Asher was feeling.

When Essie stood up, so did he. Dizziness swamped him, but after a few seconds it passed. Holding onto the counter where they'd been standing when he'd been hurt, he looked around the room. Someone must have called them all to him, because everyone was in the room now.

"I'm going with you." Before Kiaran could tell Jacob that was a bad idea, Essie did. "He's my son and I'm going with you."

"And I said no." Kiaran might have laughed, but he was sort of too busy trying not to throw up. A feeling he'd never had before either. "If you get hurt again and leave us, or she puts some of her mojo shit on you and we never see you again even in the afterlife, I will never forgive myself. We have no idea what sort of crap she can do. I can whip her ass, but not with me worrying about you."

Kiaran could see that Jacob was pissed, but he nodded. Essie helped the situation out by hugging the man tightly in her arms while she told him that she loved him too much to lose him now. Jacob sat down and held a tissue to his face. The man was worried, there was no doubt about it. And so was he.

"She must have come upon him just after I left him. I should have stayed, but I know that had she gotten us both, we might not be able to get him." Kiaran watched Essie pace as she worked things out in her head. "I'm going to kick her ass when I see her. Mark my words. And if any of you beat me to it, you're going to have to deal with me."

"I won't touch her." Zak laughed. "However, if you can see your way clear for me to kick her around a bit, I'd be much obligated to you. She hurt all of us by taking him."

Essie told him fine. As she continued to pace, Kiaran reached for Asher again. There was still a hard wall, but he knew that he was still alive. The only way he could die was if she beheaded him or stabbed him in the heart...something that he'd seen Helena do in the dream. When Essie seemed to come to a decision, he stood up. She had her game face on, a perfect description for the way her body and face were set.

"We go now. Not later when she's had time to hurt him, but right now." Casdon started to speak and she cut him off. "I need you all there with me. Without all of us, we're going to lose him. I don't want to even think about that."

"We have the element of surprise on our side." Kiaran looked at Essie as he continued. "She has no idea what sort of power you have now. Hell, it's so much I hum with it, but she won't expect it. And she has no idea that you're bringing us."

Nodding, she didn't look so sure. He started to ask her what she was thinking when he realized that she was trying to reach Asher. Putting his hands on her shoulders, he let some of the power he had move over her. He knew that Asher could connect with her, and he was completely blown away when it worked for him.

She wasn't trying to reach Asher as he'd thought, but looking into the mountain where he was. The chamber was just as he'd seen it in Asher's dream, but this time it seemed to be cleaner; the walls even seemed to shine a little. Then he realized it wasn't shining so much as it was pouring water over the large stones.

"The mountain is flooding the chambers beneath the one that they're in. He said that it will take him a few more hours, but I asked him not to stop. Asher has a better chance of swimming out of there than he would going up against her." Kiaran nodded. "I'm going to go into the dining room. I don't know if you can touch anything when I do, but help me if you can. I have to do a few things to scare some of the meanness out of Helena."

"I'll do whatever you need." They moved around the chamber. There was something else that he noticed while walking with her; someone had moved the dais. He had no idea why that was going to be important, but he made a mental note to keep an eye on it later.

As they moved into the room where she was headed, Kiaran saw Asher. He was slumped against the wall, chained there with the gold paint that had been on him before. Essie touched Asher, but she didn't disturb him as he might have.

The king was where he'd been before, with the exception that now there were fresh flowers in the vase and steaming meats and vegetables on the table. It was a feast fit for him, and Kiaran wondered where they had found some of the things there. He'd not seen dragon's cakes in a long while, and felt his mouth water for one or two. But there was work to be done, and he'd yet to figure out why Essie was here.

"I have to see who is here." She answered his unspoken question. "I need to know where all the people are and how many there are before we go in. And I want to play with her mind a little while I'm doing it."

The huge necklace that was around the king's throat was moved. He had no idea if he could have done that as well, but followed her when she laid it near Asher. Then when she returned to the table, she picked up several of the dragon's cakes and slipped them into her pocket as she picked up one of the wine glasses that was filled to near overflowing and put it in the king's hand. She had just stepped back from the king when Helena entered.

He knew the moment she saw the king's necklace. As she bent to take it from Asher, Essie bumped against the table and sent several of the other glasses tipping. When Helena turned, she looked right at them. Kiaran moved out of her way when she came at him, and it was then that he realized she was going for the king. She couldn't see them.

Helena was clearly terrified. She stared at the glass in King Ruben's fingers like he had something more heinous than a simple glass. As she backed from him, the king, Kiaran got a good look at her.

"She looks horrible." Essie nodded but said nothing. "Christ, she looks every one of her years right now. Is this what you've been doing to her?"

"Sort of. Caroline showed me how to mess with her mind. She thinks that Ruben is coming for her and that when he gets here, he's going to do all sorts of things to her.

I don't know what she thinks right now, but I've been searching her mind, looking for the best…or I guess worst, things he'd done to her when he was alive and using those thoughts against her. I don't think she's slept in a day or so."

She looked it too. When Essie told him they were leaving, he stayed with her when she talked to the mountain and then returned them to the house. He sat down, staring at the woman who would be his queen.

"You knew that he was hurting and you're going to help him." She nodded. "The mountain, has it always talked to you?"

"I think, in some way I guess." He nodded while she continued. "He's going to help us. When we get there, we'll have the path lit for us so that we won't alert her when we get to her chamber. The man of the mountain wants her gone."

"And what did he thank you for?" She flushed brightly, and he smiled. "Oh, I have to know now. Anything to make you that embarrassed."

"It's not that bad, but I had to ask the lady of the earth to help me." She got a little brighter. "Long ago he had a cherry tree on his back. I guess it wasn't really his back but the top of him. Anyway, this tree lived there and dropped her pretty blooms on his back for a long time. The fruit would bring him birds that would pick up the seeds and plant them all along the other mountains. Then one day it was killed. Someone cut it down and…. You know, I did him a favor and he's done one for us."

Kiaran laughed. It felt good, and he got up to hug her. His brothers wanted her to finish the story, but he wanted the entire complete story once they were done. And he thought that it would be a good one. As they left the house, he tried to reach for Asher again.

She wants me to summon you. He was surprised to touch Asher's mind and that he spoke to him so clearly. *Don't come here as a human. But show this bitch what happens when she fucks with our family.*

Gladly. He told Essie that he had made contact with Asher, and she nodded. *Asher, she is one scary woman, your wife. And I will gladly pledge to her if they still do that nowadays.*

I don't know what they do, but I have a feeling if you try that kind of shit with her, you might find yourself tied up next to me. He thought so too. She wasn't much on ceremony. *Keep her safe for me, Kiaran. I love her with all my heart.*

We all do, Asher. She's as much our sister as you and the others are my brothers. He told Asher to rest up, they were on their way, and he said that he would. Kiaran knew that he was still in pain because he shared it with him, but he knew that once they were together, he'd be able to heal. And Kiaran wasn't really surprised to see Elbert coming with them as a big dog.

As soon as they were in the yard, they all shifted to their dragons. He felt different than he had before; his body felt heavier, stronger even. As he took to the skies, he noticed that his wings were slightly different as well. There were horns on the tips, and his horn at his head was longer. Battle mode, he thought as he clutched Essie in his feet. He felt ready to do just about anything.

When they were at the cave entrance, he waited for the rest of them. Essie moved up to him and put her hand on his forearm. He'd not been touched by another human but Essie in this form, other than Asher, in longer than he could remember. When she pulled her hand back, he saw the mark on her own arm.

"You will be my dragon, Kiaran?" He nodded and bowed to her. "I need you to keep him safe. I know that he told you to do that for me, but I can't stand the thought of him being hurt. Watch him. You know how he'll be when the fighting starts."

"Yes. But you mustn't get hurt either." She grinned at him. "Why do I have the feeling you know just what is going to happen?"

"I do. We're going to go in there and show my mother what a force of dragons is about. And you and I are going to be...we're going to be dragon saviors." He liked that and told her so. "Good. We'll have shirts made with that on it when we're done. And pens. We'll need pens to hand out. I can see it now. People will be naming their stuffed dragons after you guys. All fluffy and stuffed, you'll sit on the end of a bed and be all nasty like."

He laughed and so did the others. He knew that she was trying to loosen their tension, and it had worked. But as soon as she turned to the mouth of the cave, he saw her draw a sword, one he'd not seen in many years. Kiaran nodded. It was fitting that she have Asher's mother's sword that had hung over the fireplace since he'd been a boy.

The cave pathway to the chamber was indeed well lit. Kiaran had no idea how the mountain was doing it, but every so often Essie would stop and put her hand on the wall. She was leaving a part of herself, giving strength to what was helping them. Kiaran had no idea how he knew this, but it seemed to click in his head. As the path widened and the ground started to level out, he realized just how deep they were. When Essie stopped at what appeared to him a solid wall, she turned to them.

"Beyond here is the chamber." Her fingers danced in the fur of Elbert, and he wondered briefly if she even knew what she was doing. "When we go in, I want you guys to surround us and make it look like you're protecting me. But when I step out in front of you, let me work. I know what I'm doing."

Kiaran had no doubt she did. They agreed that they'd do it her way to a point. Jed said that if it looked like it was going badly, all bets were off.

"Thank you, but I swear to you, I got this bitch."

Jed stood to her left, Elbert as his dog to her right. Simeon and Shane stood in front of her. Elam and Gideon stood right behind her. Kiaran and his brothers surrounded all of them. They came to the chamber wall that they needed to walk through, and Kiaran wondered how they were going to get through it, when the huge stone in front of them moved the extra few feet to accommodate them. Christ, Kiaran thought, this is going to be one hell of a showdown. And he was thrilled to be a part of it.

Chapter 13

"Chain him down. I don't want him getting up halfway through the ceremony." She looked at the wall when it began to shake. "What the hell is that?"

The stone beneath her feet shifted, and she knew that the entire wall was going to come down on top of her. As she moved back, trying to find a place to hide, if there even was one, she saw them coming into her chamber.

"Christ."

She had to agree with whomever had whispered the word, but she was too busy trying to look over her prize. Helena hadn't thought of the man calling them to him to help escape, yet here they were. All of them in their glory.

The front dragon was magnificent. He looked like he'd been carved from the very walls that held him and then covered in the finest armor. His wings when he opened them, she knew, were going to be wide, full of color, and perfectly matched to his body. She started for him, just to touch him, when he hissed at her and blew his hot breath at her feet.

"There is no need for that." She tried to sound stern, but she was in awe of them. "You'll settle down once I have you where I want you. Kneel before me, dragon beast, and pledge yourself to me."

He hissed again, his flaming breath nearly touching the hem of her robe. Fear, just a little, ran up her spine, but she stiffened herself, knowing that she was far superior to anything he had within his body.

The dragon to his left moved to stand beside the first one. He too was large, his body hard as stone, but he was a different color than the first one. He was darker with his browns and greens, fading more as it settled to his feet. Whereas the first one was standing on his hind legs, his body exposed for her to see, this one stood with his wings around him, his body compact but no less dangerous. As they moved around, forming a straight line that stood in front of her, she had a thought that she might be in trouble. They were bigger than she'd imagined them to be. And there were six of them. Taking a step back, she heard the man chained to her dais laugh.

"What's the matter, Helena the Black? Are you thinking that you might be in over your head?" He laughed again, and she looked at him. "You should know that they are going to kill you. Tear you limb from limb while you still live."

"You think I'm afraid of them?" She laughed, and even to her it sounded slightly fearful. "I have killed bigger than them with only myself against them."

She hadn't. Not even a smallish dragon that she'd found injured once. She had no idea where it had come from, but she'd convinced some of the men in the village to find it and kill it before it had taken away their children. Helena had left the village before the thing was found, fearful that it would remember her and try to kill her.

The dragons, as a whole, took a step forward, then parted in the middle. She watched as a dog — a large one without a doubt, but a dog all the same — came toward her from the opening. Helena only stared at it as he shifted and stood before her. The face, while familiar, did nothing to quell her fear.

"Helena the Black?" Helena nodded at his question. His back was ramrod straight, the sword at his side huge even considering how big he was. When he stepped forward and knelt down, stabbing his blade into the stone an inch, she thought that finally things were going her way. Then she saw her.

"Hello, Helena the Black." The way she'd said it, her voice cultured and full of hate, made Helena want to go over and slap her. But she didn't move. She wasn't even sure that she could; her feet seemed to be frozen in place. "I've come to get my husband and to kill you."

Laughter bubbled from her mouth. Even with the fear that she had, this was the funniest thing she'd ever heard. The woman only cocked a brow at her, something that nagged at her memory but was gone before she could capture it.

"You think to come into my chambers, ones that I built with my own magic, and say something like that?" The girl nodded. "And how do you plan to do that? You're nothing more...nothing more than a pampered chit that has to be waited on hand and foot."

"Really?" Helena nodded, feeling better all the time. "And what makes you think you have any claim over this chamber, as you call it? You've no power here. You have no magic so long as I have my dragons. And they are mine, in the event you didn't realize that. I can command them to do whatever I wish. You can't even get them to bow before you."

"You will see my magic." Helena reached her hands into the air to bring some of the black magic that she'd put here over the years. She pulled harder on the walls, commanding it to come to her, when she heard the girl laugh again.

"You broke your bond here." Helena started to tell her she didn't know what she was talking about when she continued. "You did well for so many years. Not taking the jewels and gems that did not belong to you. Centuries and centuries of stealing from others and leaving the coin alone. But then you got greedy and bought this."

The blue candle appeared on the dais. The man that had been there, he was simply gone. But Helena was too focused on the candle and it's meaning to think that she should be worried. There was something about it, something that she should know, but it was just lost to her. Then after several minutes, one of her coven stood beside her and spoke.

"You broke the bond by using the money to buy something for yourself." She stared at him. "I learned that from my grand mammy all those years at her knees. Never take from the table that feeds you without using it to give back. It's why she used to put pretty things on the table, like you did, so that none of the spirits would come back to get her. Then you took something for yourself, didn't you?"

Helena nodded and stared at the candle. The man who had jogged her memory tossed his robe at her and said that he was done. As soon as the words left his mouth, he disappeared in a cloud of dust. The woman tisked at her.

"You are down to nine." Looking around, she realized that three of her coven had taken off their robes. It was the only thing, full of magic from when she'd been stronger, that held them to her. The older ones, the ones from the tomb, would go to dust. The two that she'd brought to keep her number at thirteen would simply fall to the ground.

"You can't do this to me. I'm a witch of great power." The woman laughed. "Who do you think you are, coming here and destroying everything I've worked so hard to put together? Leave here now before I kill you and leave you here to rot."

"Why, Mother dear, I'm so disappointed that you don't remember me." She lifted her hands up and Helena watched as water seemed to stream from the stone and swirl around her head. The man behind the girl, the man she'd had in her chains, held her. Helena realized too late that he was adding to her power.

"My daughter would never do this to me." But she would and Helena knew it. "She was a loving daughter that worshipped me."

"Worshipped you? You have got to be kidding." Still the water moved around her, gaining not only speed but more water as she moved it. When the girl lowered her hands the water followed, shooting into the dining room as if it came from a mountain top.

Helena knew that the magic in the room was being taken apart. The table leg came rolling in the room she was in with a trail of the same water. Food—food that she'd made herself—came next; flowers, long dead and fresh, as well. She saw bones then, along with the gems and jewels that had rested on the dead for more years than the child had lived. And then she heard the screams of the coven members, their magic leaving their bodies as the magic from the room disappeared as well.

As her feet cooled with the wash of water and blackness, so did her confidence that she would come out on top. Helena looked at her daughter and tried to remember her name.

"Elsie, you can't destroy me like this. What will the other witches think when they hear what you have done?" Most of them, Helena thought, would more than likely congratulate her. "I am your mother, after all."

"It's Essie, not Elsie."

The blast of heat tore at her face. She staggered back as the big dragon blew at her again. His wings were spread out, his horns tipped, she could see now, in the finest silver. As he bent his head, she had the overwhelming urge to touch the largest horn, run her finger over the tip to see if it was as sharp as it looked. But the pain in her belly took her breath way.

He'd rammed her. Lifting her up, he shook his great head, and she knew that her belly was spilling out even as he tossed her to the wall behind her. Helena tried again for the magic that was hers, and cried out when the dragon put his clawed foot at her chest and pressed down.

"You killed my father." She tried to shake her head, to tell him she'd had no part of it, when he pressed harder into her breaking ribs and her arms. "My father was a great king. He did no one harm and you killed him."

"Ruben?" He roared then, his hot breath burning deeply into her face and body. Screaming around the pain, she begged for him to stop, telling him she was sorry for whatever he thought she'd done.

"My father was King Anthony. My mother Queen Eve." She knew it then, could see the dragon of his father in this younger one. But she knew that there had been no children from the dragons...she would have noticed. She would have made it her job to know if a child had been born of the long dead queen. "She had us a few days before you brewed the storm that destroyed so many lives. She protected us, like our father did when you sent men with swords and blades to kill him. But he won. They both won, because I will destroy you and you'll never harm another dragon as long as I live."

The claw pierced her chest. Her magic fled her then, her death as imminent as her next breath. And more than likely her last. As she lay there, her entire body burnt and blistered, some of her flesh gone to the bone, she watched as her daughter came to stand near her and wanted to beg for her life again. But nothing was working. Then the foot was lifted, but the pain, instead of going away, doubled, nay tripled, before Essie took the point of the blade and slammed it into her chest. Helena put her hand on the blade, and even though her body was dead her eyes saw what Essie did next.

Her daughter turned her back on her and walked away.

~~~

Asher held Essie as she crumbled. He held her to him as he turned them away from the burning body on the floor. There was no doubt that Helena was dead, but he wasn't taking any chances with Essie now.

When the walls began to shake again, he told the others to get out. But Kiaran told him they had to finish, it was a promise he'd made to Caroline. He told him it had to be destroyed for all time

The six dragons formed a circle. Each of them, by order of birth, stood with their backs to each other and spread their wings. When Kiaran stepped out of the circle, Elbert ran to be in the middle with his brothers and barked at him to do the same. As soon as Asher was there with Essie and his brothers, the circle closed around them.

Nothing will happen to you so long as you remain where you are. He nodded and told the rest of them what Kiaran had said. *When we finish here, you'll have to wake Essie and let her finish the rest.*

"She's hurt too." Kiaran told him he knew. "I need to get her out of here, Kiaran. She's done enough."

The two of you have to complete this, Asher. If the two of you don't do your part, what we've done here will be for naught. Asher told him he'd wake her. *Thank you. Now, don't move.*

The six of them reared up on their hind legs. When they spread their wings again, touching each to the dragon next to them, Asher knew that nothing would harm them. Then they began to spray the room with their volcanic heat, their breath burning through everything that was left of the witch and her coven.

It only took seconds for them to destroy it all. He wanted to get out of there, but they didn't move to allow them to be free. Then it occurred to him. Everything would be molten hot, and they'd be killed if they touched anything. Essie stirring in his arms brought his attention back to her. She smiled at him, and Asher felt everything was right with the world.

"Are you ready?" He nodded, then shook his head. "We have to cool it down for the mountain. I promised him we'd take care of him."

Nodding, he put her on the floor when she asked. Asher held her, wrapping his arms tightly around her as she began to reach above her head. As he watched, rain began to pour down from the chamber ceiling, hot steam hissing as it fell to the floor.

When the water began to cover his ankles, he knew what they were doing. Flooding the chamber would be the only way to keep others from coming down here. Adding his own strength to hers, the water began to flow at a faster rate, the water now up to their knees. And just when he began to worry that they'd all drown, the chamber ceiling cracked and opened, and sunlight poured in with the water. Asher knew that it would be their escape.

Kiaran picked him up and was soaring out of the chamber before Asher realized that he'd left Essie. As soon as he was on his feet, he sent the dragon back for her even as his brothers came out with their dragons. Even Elbert came out, riding on the back of Onimia and looking like he simply belonged there.

When she was lifted out, her body lowered into his arms, Kiaran shifted, as did the rest, as the opening closed around the water. Asher watched as the earth moved around the now closed opening in a way that made it look as if nothing had disrupted the area for millions of years. Just as he was going to suggest that they go home, he looked up at the cherry tree, in full bloom just beside them.

"An omen?" Kiaran told him he'd take it as such. "I think I'd like to see if we can plant a few more on the property. I had forgotten how beautiful they are this time of year."

They walked back to the house. Their father was there on the porch when they arrived, looking like a man who had been taking it easy. But the closer they got to him, the more Asher could see the lines of worry around his face. Asher hugged his dad, as did the others as soon as they were close enough to do so. Even Essie hugged him tightly to her body.

"I guess you cleaned house." He nodded at his dad as the rest of them went into the house. Elbert had told them that they would have a feast tonight in celebration. Essie stood beside him as he told his dad what had happened. "So the witch, she's dead and Kiaran killed her?"

"No, I did." Essie yawned and smiled. "If you don't mind, I think I'm going inside to take a nap before dinner. I suddenly feel like I've been working too hard."

He watched her walk to the house. Asher felt his love for her become an almost tangible thing. Asher looked at his dad when he laughed.

"You love her." Asher nodded. "Good. The two of you need each other. I think I made a good match, don't you?"

"I do." He walked with his dad to the swing that had been there for as long as he could remember, only the plank had been replaced over the years. "Dad, she was great down there. And she did what she'd told the mountain she'd do for it. Cleaned the area of all signs of the witch and her coven."

"But she killed the witch." Asher nodded, and his dad looked relieved. "I'm glad it was her. I thought for sure that Kiaran would have done it for her, but it had to be her. Were you near her when she did it?"

"I was holding her. Dad, what's going on? Why does it matter who killed her?" His dad looked so satisfied that Asher was worried. Worried enough that he wanted to go to Essie and ask her what she'd done. "Dad?"

"She'll get it all now." He asked him what he was talking about. "The power. All of it. From all of them. You'll both get it."

He still didn't understand what he meant until he remembered what Caroline had told him about Helena killing other witches to gain their powers. But Essie wasn't a witch, she was a faerie. Before he could point that out to his dad, Asher saw Caroline coming toward them.

"I thought I'd see how it went. I can feel that things went well, but I wanted to see if you needed me when things settled." Asher was becoming more and more confused by the minute. He stood up to go to Essie when he heard her scream. But before he could go to her, to protect her, his entire body felt like it had been twisted in a vise.

Crying out with his own pain, he begged his father to go to Essie. But he couldn't make him understand. Couldn't make any words pass his lips other than the screams of pain and hurt. Dropping to his knees, then his hands, Asher saw blood on the ground in front of him. All he could think about was after all this, he was going to die right here on his hands and knees.

Then as suddenly as it washed over him, it was gone. The pain in his body felt as if it had been a distant dream. Standing up, he felt weird, his body not his own. After several attempts at trying to walk, he finally got his legs to move right, his head to stay straight as he made his way to Essie.

To say he was surprised when he found her in the kitchen would have been grossly understated. But there she sat with a glass of something cold in front of her. As soon as he sat across from her, Elbert shoved a glass into his hands and told him to drink.

"I would if I were you. He threatened to tip back my head and pour it down my gullet if I didn't." Elbert huffed at her and Essie laughed. "You did. You said that you'd not have me passing out on you again."

"You scared ten years off me." Elbert pointed to his glass with a glare. "I will not let you fall again either. Drink it or I shall call your father in."

Asher drained his glass. Not that he was afraid of his father, but he was suddenly thirsty. When tea was poured into his glass again, he drank this glass a little slower. He also felt a good deal steadier on his feet when he stood up.

"What was that?" Asher told Essie he had no idea, but he was glad they were both all right. She nodded. "I felt like I was being run on the spin cycle of the washing machine, then for good measure squeezed through a pasta maker."

"Apt description. And don't forget the burn in your belly." She nodded and sipped her tea when he did. "I don't suppose we could ask someone. Like Elbert here."

"I would have told you anyway." He sat a plate of scones in front of Essie and glared at him when he took one. "The miss needs them more than you do right now. And it was the power of the coven. And those that were killed by them."

Essie ate two of the fresh scones before she spoke. Asher was eating his third one when he got up to get more to drink. He needed sweet, something that he'd never really cared for before. Getting up, he began to raid the cabinets.

"I don't have a clue what that means. I mean, I've heard of it before, like in books and stuff. *You kill the person with power and it shall come to you.*" She said this is an eerie kind of voice that made him smile. "But really. My mother, Helena, was a black witch. I'm a faerie. Why the hell would I have need of her crap? I have stuff of my own I don't know what to do with."

Kiaran came in then with a large bag from one of the local stores. He dumped the contents on the table and grabbed three of the three or four dozen candy bars, the super-sized ones, not the little bitty ones, before Asher could. He noticed that Essie took two herself, and he was eating a big bag of sweetish kinds of sour things when he started to feel like he might make it for another hour.

"You have all that they were, like you said." Caroline sat down and pointed to the empty wrappers on the table. "You crave sweets because of the fact that you're a faerie and not a witch. We would need something like a salad."

"Eww. I hate that green stuff." Elbert hit Kiaran on the back of the head when he made a face too. "I'm just...I can't seem to drink enough either. I think that is because of the flames we used. Akassa and Zak said the same thing. And so you know, I'm not a faerie. So what is up with my cravings?"

"You're all part faerie now." Asher started to shake his head when something hit him. Before he could ask, Caroline continued. "When you became...when the three of you became a family of your own, you took on traits of the rest of you. While Essie can't shift into a dragon any more than you can, Asher, she can speak to you all. And you, Kiaran, you can use the elements the same as her. The water that she poured into the cavern? That wasn't just her, you all three did it. And from now on, when one of you are hurt, happy, sad, or even just having a bad day, the other two will feel it to some degree."

"And sex?" Asher looked at Caroline instead of the other two when he asked. "I mean, when Essie and I are...you know. Will Kiaran be there as well?"

"I don't know. Has he been until now?" Kiaran said no. "Then it is doubtful that he would be now. I would say, though, that if you wish it, it would be all right. As I said, the three of you are now one."

Chapter 14

Essie was in the shower later when she thought of what Caroline had told them. They were one, and had been playing around with that fact until late last night. Their combined power was strong, and she was pretty sure that the household would never be the same again. Smiling, she thought of the little garden...well, it had been a little garden that Elbert had behind the house, and how pleased he'd been when they showed him what they'd done. She was still smiling when the door behind her opened.

"Want someone to wash your back?" She said yes and turned to face the tile as she heard Asher get in with her. "You have such beautiful skin."

Moaning when the sponge rolled down her back, Essie stretched her hands above her head to hold on. Asher was the best back scrubber in the world, and she wanted to enjoy every second of it.

"I've been thinking about what Caroline told us. About us being all one." She nodded but closed her eyes. "Kiaran thought about it too. He'd like to be with us when we have sex."

"You mean watch us?" She didn't hear what he said and turned to look at him. But it wasn't just him, it was Kiaran too. "Asher? What's going on?"

"He loves you too." Essie nodded but didn't move, only to try and cover herself up. But she watched Kiaran as he moved toward her. "I want him to touch you too. Make love to you as I do. He...you're his mate, Essie. He's known this since he met you."

"I'm your wife." Asher nodded and pulled her hands down from her breasts. He took Kiaran's hand and cupped her breast as she stood there being held by Asher. "I've never...this is very strange."

"It is, but it's right too." Kiaran leaned down and took her nipple into his mouth as Asher watched. She moaned and curled her fingers into his hair as Asher took her other breast. She was holding them to her as a hand slid down her body to her pussy. "You're wet, baby. You want this."

The water was turned off and she was pulled out of the stall. They were touching her everywhere, kissing her, fondling her. As Asher lifted her up in his arms, Kiaran kissed her. Essie thought it the most erotic thing that she'd ever had happen to her.

As she was laid out on the bed, naked and a little scared, both Asher and Kiaran stood on either side of her. She didn't know what to do. Or for that matter what to say to them.

"Do you want me?" Kiaran looked so uncertain when he asked her. "I can leave you now and I will never bring it up again. And you won't hurt my feelings if you say no."

"Do you want me?" He grinned at her and nodded to his cock. "I see. But isn't that a normal reaction when a man sees a naked woman?"

"Not with you. Not ever with you." He crawled into the bed with her and kissed her. Asher moved in on her other side and pulled her face to him, and looked at her when Kiaran pulled away.

"You all right with this? Really?" She told him she was. "Good. I'm going to enjoy this. Very much so, I think."

Her body was worshipped by them. Each of them smoothed their hands over her in places that brought her so close to coming that she cried out with it. Her breasts were suckled, bitten, then tugged almost painfully. She watched as Kiaran made his way down her body to her pussy.

"I've never done this before." She nodded and watched him. "Christ, I can smell you. I want to eat every bit of you."

"Please." He grinned and lowered his head to her pussy. Asher was behind her now, his body holding hers up while Kiaran settled between her legs. She could see every move he made.

As Asher fondled her breasts again, cupping and squeezing them, Kiaran opened her nether lips. As soon as his mouth covered her, sucking her clit into his mouth then biting her, she came, screaming out his name over and over. And every time Kiaran looked up at her, captured her eyes, she'd come all the harder when he nipped at her.

He ate her much like Asher did, like a man starved for whatever she gave him. Over and over he brought her to peak, his mouth only leaving her long enough for her to catch her breath before he was bringing her again. She was weak with it when he finally sat up. But the moment she saw his cock, thick with need and dripping long streams of precum, she felt her body respond to him.

Essie was moved around then. She was told to lean over the bed and to hold on. She did this and was pleased to see Kiaran was lying in front of her. His crown was purple, his juices making his slide up and down swift and easy. She wanted him. Badly, and she could tell that he wanted her just as much.

Asher was at her ass. His cock was between her legs but not inside of her, and she wanted that more than she wanted to breathe. But asking him to take her only had him slap her ass. Not hard, but enough to have juices run down her legs in anticipation. Essie had never had two men before, had never wanted them. But her need for these two, her love for them as well, was something that she knew was going to be right.

"We're in charge now," Asher told her as he rubbed the hot place on her ass. She nodded and licked her lips when Kiaran fisted his cock. To take him in her mouth while Asher fucked her was going to be just what she needed. Leaning down, she rolled her tongue around his crown and tasted his precum. It was hot, hotter than Asher's, but it was delicious. Taking him into her mouth, she sucked hard, rolling her tongue around him when Asher entered her.

Nothing would have prepared her for the sensation of two men. Both of them well endowed, both of them in love with her, filled not just her body but her heart as well. As she moved her hand to cup Kiaran's balls, Asher slid his fingers into her pussy as he fucked her harder. She was so close to coming that when she tasted Kiaran's come filling her mouth, she cried out with her own release, tightening around Asher as he pounded her hard through his own. The second climax she had, this one blowing her head off, she was sure, took her body apart and slammed it back together twice before darkness took her.

~~~

Kiaran held her to his body. Asher was curled around her back, and he wrapped his arm around him as well. They were a family, and more than that, they were going to be together for a very long time. He wondered if his brothers would find mates in the men that they protected as well. He was thinking about that when Essie touched her fingers to his forehead.

"You're thinking too hard." He kissed her then; taking her mouth came as natural to him as breathing. "That is a wonderful thing to wake up to, but what has you worried so much?"

"My brothers, their mates." She nodded and moved over his body, Asher rolled to his back as well. "You're making me very hard again."

"You are already hard. I felt it on my leg and it woke me up." She rocked her hips over him, and he moaned when she touched her fingers to his cock. "I'd like to ride you. I enjoy that every much."

"What about Asher?" She sat up over his hips, and he held his cock for her. As she slid down over him, Kiaran felt his eyes roll to the back of his head. "Christ, you feel good."

She rocked over him, a slow cant that made him want to both come in her and make it last forever. Essie took his hands and cupped them to her breasts, showing him what she wanted. He rocked his hips up and down with hers, and watched her face as pleasure seemed to show in every part of her.

"Suck my nipple, Kiaran. I want to come, and you fucking me like this is going to bring me." Sitting up, he did as she wanted. His cock felt deeper this way, and he held her ass to him as she rode him hard and quick. "I'm coming."

Her shout had him rolling her to her back so that he could come with her. Asher was awake now, and he was fisting his own cock when he leaned in and kissed Essie. He came then, filling her body with his cum even as he felt Asher come on his back. Kiaran came again when Asher did, his body bowed back over Essie as she screamed again.

Kiaran rolled off her when Asher touched him. He was between her legs even as Kiaran felt his cock harden again. Watching them, seeing them together like this, had him fisting his cock, and knowing that it was her cum that was making him sticky had him coming quickly after the two of them.

"I love you." Essie kissed Asher, and Kiaran felt a little jealous. Then she turned to him. "And I love you too. Very much. I feel complete now. Not that I didn't with just Asher, but now...well, now it seems as if I'm whole. I've never felt this way before."

"Me neither." He hadn't either. "I knew what you were to me...from the start. But I was...no one wants to be rejected, and once I figured out that Asher was your mate, or husband too, I was ready to leave for a while. Seeing the two of you like you are now, it was too much. Painful, if you must know."

Asher leaned on his hand, and with Essie between them they talked. Asher told them that he'd thought of Kiaran in bed with them. Not sexually for him; he had no desire for that for now, but he loved watching him make love to Essie.

"She's enjoying this as much as I am. It's wonderful and fulfilling, like she said." Asher kissed her, and Essie put one of her hands on each of their cheeks and nodded. Asher continued. "I don't know if we'll both have sex with you nightly, but I would like for us all to sleep together.

I've been…Kiaran has been a part of me for my entire life, and I'd like for him to be a part of yours too."

"Of course. But we'll need a bigger bed. And a bigger room. By the way, are we staying here?" Kiaran had never thought of that. If they left here, he'd be a dragon all the time. And the only way he'd be able to sleep with them was as a part of Asher. "Kiaran?"

"I can be wherever you are." She could see that he wasn't telling her all, and when she pulled his face to hers, he confessed his thoughts.

"Then we stay here. If you want?" Essie looked at Asher. "We can build a house that we can all live in, or stay here. But I want Kiaran with us."

"I agree. We can enlarge this room." He waved his hands and the room seemed to expand. Kiaran had forgotten that he could do that, make things with his magic. "And the bed is no problem."

The bed didn't double but tripled. There was plenty of room for them to sleep together, and even make love if they wanted. Kiaran pulled Essie to him and kissed her. Asher wrapped around them and they all laid there for several moments before Essie spoke again.

"I want a child with you guys." Kiaran felt his heart start to beat faster in his chest. "I'm not sure how this will work, or even if it will. But I want us to have a baby together and give it the best of what we have."

"When?" Asher yawned as he continued. "I'd like to wait until we can get settled here first. My businesses can be run from anywhere. All I need to do is update the Internet service here and bring in someone to help in the office. Kiaran, what do you think? Want to have a child with this woman?"

He did. "More than anything in this world." He put his hand on her belly and felt the tightness of it, and wondered if it was possible that she'd look any more beautiful than she did right now. "Yes, whenever you are ready, we'll make a child together."

When they were both asleep, Kiaran got up. He was pulling on his boots when someone entered the kitchen. He looked up at Zak when he sat down. When he was finished, he looked at his younger brother.

"She's your mate." Kiaran nodded. "I thought so. Do you think that's going to be true for the rest of us?"

"I have no idea. I think so. I mean, I don't know how else it would work if she wasn't." Zak nodded. "Are you okay with that?"

"I am, I think. I mean, I have some thoughts on it. I've never...what is sex like?" Kiaran grinned. "That good, huh?"

"Better." He stood up. "I'm going to take a walk and fly for a bit. Do you want to come with me?"

"Nah. But I would like to ask that you soundproof your room. I'm right next door with Jed, and you guys are a little on the noisy side." Kiaran flushed and Zak laughed. "I'm teasing you. I didn't hear anything until you came down the stairs. I just wanted to...I'm worried it won't be that way for the rest of us. To be so much in love that you're willing to share."

"We're not sharing, not really. We're...Essie and Asher said that we're one. I think that's about right. And when we're together, it's not like we're three people making love to one person; it's all of us enjoying each other."

"You and Asher have sex?" It wasn't shocked sounding, but Zak did look concerned. "I'm not sure I feel that way with Jed. I love him, but not sexually."

"No. Asher and I don't have sex with each other. But we did have it with Essie. And she's amazingly...she's just amazing." Zak nodded and stood up too. "We're going to be staying here. Asher is moving his part of the business here tomorrow."

"I think Jed wants to stay too. He's been talking about it with Shane and Simeon. They think they'd like to be here too. Closer to their mom and all. I'd like to be where I can see Mom and Dad too. Plus, I have it in my head to try and rebuild the castle with them."

"That's my plan as well." Zak nodded but before he left, Kiaran said his name. When he turned, Kiaran continued, "She loves me. Very much. She said that being with us completes her."

"I think I'd like that feeling as well. But we'll see." Kiaran nodded. And when Zak left him, he went into the yard.

It took him nearly an hour to get to the cave where his mother was. He'd stopped to look at the view from a lot of vantage points along the way, and really looked at the earth surrounding him. He sat on one of the stones nearest her and looked at what she'd done for them. Not the gold and gems, but how she'd protected them.

"I have a mate." It didn't seem as weird talking to her as he'd thought it would be. "She's Asher's mate as well. You'd like her. She's mouthy and funny. Smart and very strong. She'd have to be to put up with us."

He grinned when he thought of her tangling with Jacob. "She's not one you'd call a pushover either. Jacob is kinda in awe of her too."

Kiaran told her about how Jacob had come to be with them again. And he told her about the witch and how they'd all worked together ridding the world of her. He also told her of his plans to rebuild the castle with the rest of them, and couldn't wait to see it standing.

He was standing to leave, feeling really good about talking to her, when something caught his eye. Kiaran moved to see what it was and was surprised to find a book. It looked to be as old as he was. Sitting down, he looked at the pages that had been painstakingly drawn with such detail that he could see the castle in all its glory.

There were drawings of tapestries and paintings of his parents. Furniture was drawn out, along with how high it had to be, the length to fit in certain places, and which room it had been in. None of the sizes meant much to him — they were measured in reference to a man named Conway — but Kiaran knew someone that could help.

Fireplaces were drawn out, with extra detail given to the stone that covered it, the hearth that was resting in the grate, as well as how many cords of wood it would need to burn it through a cold night.

As he looked through the pages, telling his mother what he was going to do with each one, he felt like he was going to bring things back to life that had long since been forgotten. He even explained to his mom what things they'd have to add to the castle when it was finished to make it more modern for them, bring it to this century, but in a way that wouldn't distract from the beauty of the castle itself.

There were pictures of dress of both women and men, of servants and horse men. In the back there were names of farmer who had helped them, and the person who had painted the portraits. Even a list of the magic that had been used to make the rooms safe, the castle walls stronger, and the candles burn so they would not catch the curtains on fire was included.

"Mom, this is going to be wonderful. Thank you so much for this." He stood up then and walked to where she held his egg in her hand, knowing that she had somehow made it so he'd find it now. "I wish with all my heart I could have known you. Could have been held by you that I could remember. Not a day goes by that I don't think of you. What you had to suffer to make sure we were safe. You and Dad...there is no other parent like you two. And you did a good job finding Jacob and Sally to...oh Mom, I love you so very much."

Kiaran touched the sigil on his arm and felt tears fall. As they did, he captured them, thinking of what he'd do with the gems as he held them. He was going to have a bracelet made for his mates. One for Essie and one for Asher.

As he left the cave, he felt lighter. The book was tucked under his arm and he couldn't wait to show it to the rest of them. But instead of going home, he made his way to the castle ruins. He needed to see it alone this time.

His father and mother had given their lives for them. He moved around the one standing wall and put his hand to it. The feelings he got from it, the warmth of love, made him realize that his dad, as much as his mom, had given him the book to follow.

"We're going to bring it back. Maybe find you in the process. I'd like to...I think I'd like to take you to Mom if we can. I think you should be together, don't you?" Kiaran thought he heard the building sigh, and he nodded. "We'll find some part of you, Dad, and take you to be with Mom. It's only right after all this time."

Kiaran walked back to the house now. It was full daylight when he stepped into the kitchen, and wasn't really surprised to find Elbert there. He sat a plate of food in front of him almost as if he'd been expecting him. Kiaran looked up at him, taking his hand in his before he could move away.

"You've been a good friend to us, Elbert. Almost like a father." The man squeezed his hand and nodded. "Thank you for being there for us. I don't think we tell you that often enough."

"You don't, so take care that you do. And Jacob, he needs it more than me." Kiaran nodded. "She's your mate now? You've bonded with her?"

"Yes." He looked up at him when he walked away. "You knew? You knew that Essie was my mate?"

Elbert turned and looked at him. "Well, of course I did. I've been around a good bit longer than you, young man, and I know a thing or two."

When he turned his back to him, Kiaran laughed. Christ, he'd not felt this good in a very long time. And he was happy that he'd come with Asher all those weeks ago. Life, he thought as he dug into his breakfast, was going to be fun from here on out.

Join our Newsletter & Receive Release Day Announcements, News, and Special Sales!

Just go to our website and click on the link.

Before You Go...

Share your voice and help guide other readers to these wonderful books. Even if it's only a line or two your reviews help readers discover the author's books so she can continue creating stories that you'll love. Login to your favorite retailer and leave a review.

Kathi Barton, author of the bestselling series Force of Nature, lives in Nashport, Ohio with her husband Paul. In addition to writing full time Kathi likes to spend time with her eight grandkids, three children and three children-in-laws. She writes to relax and have fun.

Her muse, a cross between Jimmy Stewart and Hugh Jackman brings them to life for her readers in a way that has them coming back time and again for more. Her favorite genre is paranormal romance with a great deal of spice. You can visit Kathi on line and drop her an email if you'd like. She loves hearing from her fans. aaronskiss@gmail.com.

Follow Kathi on her blog:
http://kathisbartonauthor.blogspot.com/

www.ingramcontent.com/pod-product-compliance
Lightning Source LLC
Chambersburg PA
CBHW032123170626
46808CB00006B/2086